THE SMELL OF WET BRICKS

FICTION: 9

The Smell of Wet Bricks, 3rd Edition

By Chiya Parvizpur

Copyright © 2024 Transnational Press London

First Published in 2024 by Transnational Press London in the United Kingdom, 13 Stamford Place, Sale, M33 3BT, UK.

www.tplondon.com

Transnational Press London® and the logo and its affiliated brands are registered trademarks.

Requests for permission to reproduce material from this work should be sent to: sales@tplondon.com

Paperback

ISBN: 978-1-80135-273-4

Digital

ISBN: 978-1-80135-274-1

Cover Design: Nihal Yazgan

Cover Image: Painting by Wria Parvizpur

Transnational Press London Ltd. is a company registered in England and Wales No. 8771684.

The Smell of Wet Bricks

Chiya Parvizpur

3rd Edition

TRANSNATIONAL PRESS LONDON

2024

Every word of this story is dedicated to Shima Adib, my brother Worya Parvizpur, Akbar Mansuri and Erfan Shahyad, whose paintings have impregnated my words with sublime feelings; and also my uncle, Attar Salimi, whose real life is a surrealistic novel.

CONTENTS

ABOUT THE AUTHOR

Chiya Parvizpur is a Kurdish author born in Sanandaj, the Kurdistan of Iran. He plays Tamura and teaches English for a living. Having studied English Literature with the intention of writing creative works of fiction in English, he opts for reviving his folk culture, myth, and history. In this way, he desires to unearth erstwhile pangs that would otherwise remain veiled and repressed in the labyrinths of time and place. First edition of his debut novel, *The Smell of Wet Bricks* was published in 2017 by Transnational Press London.

A Letter to God

Thereafter the suffocation of Halabja,
I wrote a long letter
To God.
Before anyone else,
I read it to a tree.
The tree wept,
And thereunder
A letter-carrier bird said,
'Who is to deliver it?
If waiting for me to take it,
I won't get to the throne of God.'

Night neared and it was late.
The dressed-in-black angel of my poetry said,
'Don't grieve anymore,
I'll take it for you,
Up there,
To the galaxy,
But I give no promise whatsoever,
That God himself will get the letter,
You know,
Who sees God Almighty?'
'Thanks. You do fly,' said I.
The angel of inspiration flew
And took the letter.
The day after, it came back.

The fourth-ranked secretary of the office of God,
An Obayd-named,
On the same letter,
At footnote,
In Arabic,
Has written back to me:
Hey you
Fool fellow
Do translate it into Arabic
No one speaks Kurdish in here
And we too will take it not to God.

Sherko Bekas

1

The window is gently opening.

A floating dark cloud comes into view through the half-opened wooden window. It is opening, and the rocks express themselves at the heart of the mountain. Oak trees have sprouted among the stones and rocks. The scene is wide open, and the oak jungle emerges throughout the mountain; it abounds with never-perishing oak trees that challenge mortality. If others blast them, they will turn green again; if others burn them, they will spring forth again; if others attempt to uproot them, they will grow beneath the earth, revive, and spread once more. These are trees that defy death and have become the graveyard of myths.

Beneath the shade of a weathered oak tree adorned with newly-sprouted buds, an old-looking girl stands by a grave, engrossed in reading a notebook. This notebook possesses pages of white paper that shall never know completion; its words perpetually intertwine, birthing new stories that lovingly embrace the untold tales of the land of the Kurds.

Suddenly, as she becomes aware of the encroaching darkness and the wind that cloaks the surrounding jungle, her yearning to visit the Room of Inspiration ignites. This room holds the promise of reviving her withered wellspring of creativity. After absorbing every word within the notebook, her determination to venture there solidifies.

Amidst this ambiance, the haunting and howling voices of two brothers, each holding a Tembur in hand, resonate like the mournful cry of the wind through twisting valleys. Their melancholic song dances among the trees, weaving its way through branches until it reaches the ears of the girl. This lamenting melody, accompanied by the gentle intonation of the Tembur, entwines itself with the girl's heart, merging her essence with that of the earth.

Wind plays with the creaking window. In the dimness, the girl's flickering eyes make a conspicuous appearance. Her tearful eyes shed drops that she wipes away, and with each tear, an idea seems to detach from her mind—an idea with the potential to revolutionize the world. This is a world that has averted its gaze to ignore the genocide of the Silent City.

The black Cat appears in the window, its giant body occupying a considerable portion of the frame. Step by step, it crosses its regular path. So piercing are its eyes that they can metamorphose anyone. Their light conveys a mysterious fear. As the cat settles on the edge, a strong wind starts to blow, the insouciant sun sets, and its torturing rays fade into black. Night arrives, and the clock freezes at 11:11.

The roots of trees cradle a dead body in their arms, granting it a semblance of immortality. These trees have anchored their roots so deeply into the earth that not even earthquake could shiver the dead body's steadiness. So elevated is his grandeur that even nature is sucking the nectar of his essence dry. Though his earthly vessel rests below ground, the surrounding mountains, nurtured by his presence, soar skyward. Day by day, as they pierce the sky and rise ever higher, these rock-ribbed mountains grow more audacious and bold, wild enough that any gazing eye might be scratched.

Amidst this landscape, there stands a sole dried oak tree-- the very one positioned over his body.

2

Omar Kawar: The Sixth Narrative

With the birth of the Brothers of Time, the people of the Silent City became the creators of death. They ceased mourning for the departed, including the mother of the Brothers of Time, who herself passed away shortly after giving birth to them. Amidst a profound and meaningful sense of relief, they acknowledged this truth. They refrained from speaking of it openly, yet they maintained an unwavering grasp on its reality.

The sunlight became an irritant to their eyes, but the tranquillity of night and its shroud of darkness provided inspiration. During nights, accompanied by the soothing breeze, within the realm of darkness, they delved deep into their beings, playing music as they readied themselves for the promised night ahead.

Venturing through the dark expanse of the night, they danced to the rhythm of life beneath a canopy of stars, deliberately avoiding the harsh touch of the sun's rays. With the birth of the Brothers of Time, the melody of music resurfaced, taking root within people's hearts and fingertips. As night descended, the Sar Tarz Maqam would infuse new life into their weary bodies, akin to the inaugural ecclesiastical melody that accompanied the dawn of humanity; in those primordial moments when the human form was shaped from clay, the soul awaited the breath of life. Thus, nature and angels employed this melodic cadence, which the human body accepted in rapt surrender. With the performance of the Sar Tarz Maqam, the human spirit soared, enveloped in a euphoric self-transcendence.

Their perspective on life underwent a profound transformation. They played Tembur more ardently, recited Kalam, their sacred books, more passionately, and utilized language in a different fashion. They desired to alter the meaning of everything in that they figured out the power of words could flutter their history. They taught their children the art of discerning the scent of wet bricks; that way, in future, they could reclaim their *Nishtiman*, their cherished motherland, and expel the presence of colonizers.

I look at my wrist watch, it is fall. The oak trees release a cascade of yellow and brown leaves onto the slopes of the valleys. The hour hand of my watch spins so swiftly, and it suddenly stops moving. I raise my head and see myself in a mirror; wrinkled lips, white hairs, and a long grey beard of mine are beyond the horizon of my understanding. It is as if a hundred years have passed. Now, it is winter and the white coldness obligatorily moves everyone inside their houses.

I am standing at Omar Kawar's house, and I realize that a colorful fish has replaced his head, and snake-like scales have covered his body. His seven daughters are changing the Tamura strings and wrapping their instruments in green cloth. The Brothers of Time are warming the Dafs' skins upon the heat of the fireplace. All the people of Silent City are tuning up their instruments. Everybody has gone to bath, and the fragrant aroma of their bodies drenches the air; women and girls are making up their faces with pomegranate.

"Here comes the promised night", Omar Kawar whispered into my ears.

Just the Brothers of Time and Omar can see me. Abruptly, I am thrown into a phantasmagorical atmosphere in which there is no clear-cut boundary between things. Oak trees, mountains, and stones are interwoven, and I can see people who stitch their lips and dribble their blood under the oak trees. After the sunset, all people with their Tanburs and Dafs gather around the biggest oak tree located at the center of their city's square.

The dried oak tree has fruited apples, big rotten apples.

Some people are going through the oak jungle to take children beyond the highest mountain, so they can put them in a safe space. They are sleeping in their arms. There exists a deep, large, and hollow space resembling a bowl surrounded by stony mountains and thick oak trees. They put the children there, because they don't want them to see scenes which might be beyond their comprehension. I can see them all inside the hole. They are shining as a bunch of cats' eyes at night. They pour oaks on them and cover them all with leaves and branches of trees. After covering the leaves with soil, they come back.

The children are under the earth, but their weeping screams, through the trees, reaches the ears of a skinny girl with long hairs and big eyes standing upon a grave under a dried oak tree. She is reading a notebook. Their crying is blended with the ardor of people's music. The Brothers of Time invite the girl to join the Sama and Dhikr circle.

Women, men, the old and the young are playing Daf and Tanbur, and the mountains quiver; they are playing Sar Tarz, Jelaw Shahi, and Balwashan Maqams. The entire universe is trembling in the bowl of their Tanburs, and the entire nature is dancing with the movement of the strings.

They are giving their long hairs to the wind. They stand on a ground beneath which is the graveyard of their myths, a place in the heart of earth where has been always sheltered by thousands of snakes. But now with the peak of music and dance, from the depth of it, a spurt of black oil is erupting and drizzling over people.

Some of them, who are sitting around the tree, with speedy and sequential Golriz and two-finger Riz strokes, play Tanbur so heartily fast that the instruments, due to the blaze of the strings, get afire. The Tanburs are burning; the Dhikr prayers are burning. While burning, all people are dancing; while dancing, all people are burning. With the up-and-down movement of their heads, tiny fire flames are drizzling on roofs, balconies, and yards. Fire is raining, and people are burning and turning.

Wind blows and pours their ashes on mountains. The Silent City seems dark like a vague dream.

I heard the sound of bombers approaching the city. They were tearing the sky apart. The whole city's sky got black as if a bunch of crows were flying over the city to migrate south.

The bombing scene seemed ridiculous. Before bombs hit the ground, they all had been burnt in the fire of music notes. Nobody was there since they had returned back to Mother Earth.

11

3

His life was not empty of excitement; never did he have a monotonous life, and, even now that his body lies in a corner thereunder a tree, never will he be immune from menace. Wanderer, nomad, homeless, or whatever you may call him will not make a change in his path, since he is an emperor. Nothing else matters to him except for his mission. He holds an unswerving grip on freedom, and is similarly unburdened by any form of blame. Having embraced the essence carried within the scent of wet bricks, he committed himself to breaking down the barriers and setting forth on a journey of self-discovery, a voyage into a self that had been fractured into pieces, mirroring his motherland which had also been divided and shattered.

His life centers around a cemetery located at the bottom of a high mountain at the north-most part of a jungle abounding with oak trees. His mind does not encroach on another site; his thought is not completely dried up but limited to his dark but soothing residence. The oak jungle is deeply rooted in his mind, and his one-and-only confidant is his oak tree which shelters him from the scorching and the torturing light of the sun and the drops of snow. Coming of the night is what he desires to give him the opportunity to approach his true self; it is what Melek Taus, the god of languages, has predetermined for him.

Myriads of snow crystals are nauseatingly and slowly descending upon the earth. Waves of snow, blended with the yellow light of the lights, create a dimly dream-like atmosphere where boundaries cease to exist. Indifference and motionlessness have seeped into the bodies of those residing outside the jungle, people who live in ignorance of the day. They sleep fourteen hours a night and murder words nonstop when awake. However, never do they think of what happened to them, or never do they direct their way astray into the jungle; those people who do not know and never bother to think to understand or they know and sell their dead victims in exchange of a petite sum; those who close their eyes and change their manners and walk away from their ground. They will never get to know the secret of wet bricks.

Thereunder a tree at the heart of jungle, there exist two spook-like creatures whose power of imagination and delicate hearts have inundated their surrounding space. Their fancy falls over the branches of trees like sparkling frosts. The trees, the bushes, and even the dried flowers covered in snow sway with their spiritual vibe. Their power converts the cruel and cold howl of wind, which sleds amongst thick branches of the jungle, into a sad but, at the same time, horrifying music.

Resho is lost in thoughts of his girl; his possessions reduced to the mere pen in his hand and a pocketful of cigarettes. He contemplates the quest that smoking each cigarette bestows upon him, along with the sensation of ascending into the skies through the movements of his pen on the notebook. He has undergone numerous adventurous ups and downs to the extent that he now feels as if he's losing both place and time.

Long, dark locks of hair cling together as they fall onto his sunburnt arms. His eyes, with their multiple hues, linger deep within their sockets, while his emaciated body moves with reluctance. He appears transfigured, akin to the leafless trees in the cold winter. Conversely, his friend (His friend? Who is he? Could that be me?) has descended into a deep slumber for the past three days, remaining motionless like a lifeless log resting upon the surface of a tranquil lake.

The pitter-patter and click-clack of melting snowdrops echo throughout the jungle. As the sun emerges, Resho seeks refuge beneath an oak tree, hands pressed over his ears. He trembles, resembling the catatonic branches of lifeless trees swaying amidst wild winds. A gust sweeps by, compelling the trees to sing a haunting tune. The labyrinthine trails of the jungle multiply, leaving Resho with no escape. He retraces his steps, calling out to his friend, but his calls meet only silence. Placing his left arm over his shoulder, Resho begins to speak to his friend, all while jotting down his thoughts within his notebook:

I can tell you these stuff now that you are asleep and can't hear me. Since I did my mission, and Tawuse Melek, The Peacock Angel, got his nose out of my dreams, I wanted to return to myself, and I opted out of the rat race. Always wanted to be the emperor of every kind of feeling—pure and real ones. Now I reign over fear. I do fear. I fear the light. A while later, maybe, I be the emperor of happiness. This is what I've always dreamt of; living and being lonely within and without myself, my vulnerably helpless self. Two days ago, you were still asleep; I took a bath in the public restroom down there, like a newly-born child. Some people that were there got a gander at me; mocked me, laughed at me; and pitied on me, but I pitied them as well. I pitied them because they are all happy and not sad; after the genocide of the Silent City, all Kurdistan should weep and grieve. I pity them for the scars on their soul and body are healed and their silence is indeed tormenting the dead. I can't get along with a person other than myself. I don't mean you dude, you are something special. Maybe we are one. I plucked up the courage to walk out on my girl because she wanted me to be hers, not mine. To look on the bright side, this event removed the distance between me and my self, and I always thank her for that. The day I abandoned everything, she told me she would meet me under my oak tree exactly the next year. I think tomorrow is the day. After paying back my debt to Melek Tawus the god of languages and the children of Silent City, and writing my dreams about Omar Kawar and his nation, my mind got relieved. I could no longer cheat myself by living inside society. I chickened out. I decided to stick to myself and hold my grip tight on it. I newly came here and a cold wind was blowing. A torn piece of newspaper was moving with the wind. I caught it. I read it. I realized that a bitter truth was lurking under the surface of my life. Every inch of my life is written by by Melek Taus, the god of the blue. I never tried to change anything. I was way thrown into an ocean of tranquillity. After reading that article in the newspaper, he no longer came to my dreams. To make a long story short, it argued that our mind sends a ray about one hundredth of a second into the future, so you get the impression of that place as something seeming familiar. You got the point? Come on comrade, wake up and give it a thought. Figuring out this truth has darkened my life to death. It is frightening, really frightening. It gets you down, down-to-earth where you are. This means nothing is in your control. It means destiny sits there in the dark waiting for you, yet invisible to the mortal's eyes. At the end of the day, I helplessly admitted it. Oh fate, oh damned fate, it was my greatest enemy, and now I get along with it. This is me and my future is there. I used to talk to it at nights. I felt it was hiding behind the trees; I followed it, smelt it, and tracked its footprints; I could feel it as clear and tangible as the children of Silent City. I craved to ask it to cast me into the next ten years to witness the result of my mission. Being my enemy or not,

15

it is there on the bench waiting for me to play chess together. Hey dude, I am sort of happy that my destiny is written to be beside you at this point. We can't be wicked for we have tasted darkness from within. You yourself created me and you were unknowingly haunted by me. Sleep comrade, sleep. I really do envy you. It is for a month or so that I didn't get a good sleep. The screams of the dead don't let me sleep.

He opens his eyes. The darkness of the night has cloaked the lights. He genuflects and ignites a cigarette. The smoke rises slowly in rhythmic waves, ascending into the sky. It carries Resho backward in time—to the university, his home, the children of Silent City, the mission bestowed upon him by the god of inspiration, to Omar Kawar, his paintings, and his beloved girl. As the cigarette meets its end, he descends once more into his notebook.

Needy are us all, needy of something to emancipate us from the truth. When I stepped inside the jungle, I gave myself a word to take a lifelong sojourn here. This is the due place of obtaining which I always dreamt. This is Eden itself away from knowledge and here is my shelter. Its seclusion leaves a contusion on my mind, yet it is full of relief. The more I be with people, the farther I get from myself. This idea of detachment soothes me while for others it seethes them in fury. Here sounds different, and I am from here. The world outside gives me feelings and needs of other sorts—used and second-hand. Looking at other people eating, quenches my hunger; watching lovers walking hand in hand, bestows on me the feeling of being with my girl. These are the unreal reals. I experience reality in illusion, and this is the nature of universe. This jungle may be no more than a dream; perhaps I am him, and, today, my being three days of not awaking.

Can you hear? It's the call of my tree, summoning me once more. This time, there's something she wishes me to know. Her melancholic call is sensuous. It's different now, a sensation that clouds my thoughts. My body and soul ache with a hunger to heed her call, even though fear grips me. Yes, I'm afraid this time, friend. The question lingers: What does she want from me? This fear, it's overwhelming, a consuming terror.

She has always been so welcoming to me even now that she is dried up. I feel she is the Malik Tawus incarnate— he who doomed me, he whose cruel determination sacrificed me. However, I am delighted I was the one chosen to immortalize the children of Silent City. Euphoric am I that their voice will be echoing in the corners and narrow alleys of history. But no one hears them, do they?

She has shown me the truth and darkened my whole life; I always loved darkness.

The Brothers of Time are there beside my tree with their Temburs in their hands. I wonder how they step into my world. Their presence seems so soothing but at the same time heavy. When I see them, slumber or awake, I, on the spur of the moment, feel Malik Taus, the god of colors, catatonically sitting on my mind. As always, they ceaselessly sing the song of sorrow. They elegize the dead. As soon as I heard their song for the first time in my dream, I felt the weightiness of thousands of years of history bottled up on my shoulders. I don't understand them. I wish I could find out what they want to tell me. Oh my girl, I know that I'll die today or tonight and you'll find this notebook on my dead body. I want to tell you something so you can understand me better while you are reading it.

Their voice is deafeningly-but-at-the-same-time-mellifluously beyond belief. If you ever dare to go into a deeply dark valley located beneath a mountainously high mountain, feel the frightening altitude of mountains mingled with the howl of the wind, and, out of the blue, confront an oak tree thereunder which there exists an open grave with a dead body inside seeming alive and singing a sad song with no words, you will better understand my sublime fear of their elegy chant.

I stagger among the visible waves of their voice to reach them, but they vanish, and I dissolve into my oak tree.

There has appeared a puddle under my old oak tree. Agitated am I, so agitated. Thereafter the demise of my tree, birds have left us marooned as if the universe is indemnifying against the leaflessness of my tree. My one and only tree is lonely, but its seclusion has attracted me. It is leafless and fruitless, but it has firmed its roots inside the heart of earth. All these trees are of my tree's roots, yet it is itself dried up. I approach, lean on its trunk, and gaze into the puddle that has appeared underneath it. I behold my face in it. It seems to me like a mirror and even beyond that, it reflects my whole life. It embodies my bygone days and nights, my fears, my future, my repressed desires, my girl, the black Cat and the children of Silent City. The puddle swallows my words even those lingering in the deep layers of my unconscious mind.

Which truth is it going to reveal? Agitated am I, so agitated.

17

A dark cloud veils the sky. I'm tracking down the first drop falling into the puddle. All my dreams circularly swirl over the surface. Drops of rain break all the images and words, and together with the drops, they penetrate through the ground. Earth is being frozen, and the weather is getting cold. Now the puddle seems clearly see-through, completely still and waveless. Is this me? I can't believe my deep and sunken eyes, wrinkled lips, white hair, and long bleached beard.

It is as if hundred years have passed.

An image appears in the mirror of the water. Two leaders of two countries are signing a document inside a room as they are whipped by their big master. They are laughing. A number of dirty beggars enter the room and sign the document with the blood on their fingers. The document is all red. The beggars go out and they multiply while leaving. They become three hundred or so gunners. They cover their faces by anti-chemical-gas masks and put syringes in their pockets. The people of Silent City decide to leave their city but the gunners block their way. They are forced by bullets to return to their houses and take shelter in the basements. It is so cold outside and they do as they were told. Bombers appear in the sky and drop chemical bombs. The smoke is white, the smell is sweet. The heavy gas goes straight down into the basements.

My Melek Taus, oh my stone-hearted god, I am breathing my last breaths. Tell me why you are showing these images to me now?

God, help me. I'm feeling my immediate death yet I can't understand the meaning of those images. My thoughts only reach the territory of my death and I'm sure it's close. Sirwan? Where are you Sirwan? This responsibility should fall on your shoulders ...

I still don't know what the god of inspiration wants from me. I feel his reason for choosing me was writing the story of the people of Silent City. He didn't come to my dreams since I had surrendered them to the eternity of words.

The flickering of the stars

Opens and closes my eyes.

I remember

My only star

That set

18

And had my destiny moved.

The dark stars on my shoulder

Are marching,

And turn my shoes into a fountain of blood,

My fingers.

Nauseatingly are moving the clock hands,

Time sits on the shell of an old turtle.

I have the vision,

I behold,

Clear and bright,

The invisible hand behind the wheel of time

Aiming at the resurrection of my death.

I hear

The terrifying howl of an ant

Fell in a drop of water

Pondering that

The entire world has gone with the flood.

Its waves of desire I can feel,

And the scream of its horn

Summons the universe

To dry every inch of

My cells

My mind

My imagination.

The nature's insouciance

Has granted me insanity

As if she wants my body

To be a bait

For the trees.

I look at my watch. It is winter. I sit under my tree watching the sunset beyond the mountains. The last rays of the sun, like cold arrows, are being thrown to separate directions, and I am still restless.

I can hear booms, roars, and screaming people who are running towards the mountain. Their voices are more horrifying than the color of the victims. Oh the god of death and resurrection take my life since I can no longer bear the weight of life.

A young boy made it to the top and walked down the other side of the mountain towards me. His clothes were all wet. It seemed he fell into a puddle of water. His body was burnt, his skin sizzled. The gas was burning his eyes and he couldn't see. He became blind. His mouth leaked some words. All his nine siblings together with his parents were killed in their basement. He sought help. Fire was ablaze inside and outside his body. He fell on the ground. Language was broken in his tongue and he couldn't speak in one piece. He wanted to utter his last words. I lowered my head near his mouth.

"All. Sacrificed. For. The. Sake. Of. Some. Images. So. They. Could. Stop. The. War." The young boy said then fell breathless.

I quickly ran to gather some woods. I made a fire then brought him some water. He drank it and life reluctantly came back inside his body. "We thought," he kept talking, "those who'd promised to protect us from the others would really take care of us. But they didn't let us escape. Can you imagine? They let their friends and family die. People knew well that the city will be bombarded. We wanted to run away but they made us return. They had masks. They knew about the chemical bombs and they let us burn. They were shooting us so we had to rush back to our houses. Then there came the chemical and explosive bombs. All my family died before my eyes and the chemical gas blinded my eyes. It was the doom day. I could feel, I could hear that men and women, old and young, were trampled underfoot. I could hear with my own ears that mother threw away their babies so they could run away. No one knew what they were doing. I heard the doomsday. So much better that I went blind. What if I saw those scenes?" He died after uttering those words.

Melek Taus, are you torturing me? What did I write? What was my real mission? Why didn't I know? Why did I trust my imagination? I won't forgive myself. Oh, the god of inspiration, was it my fault or yours? Take my life but don't let my whole life, my thoughts, my writings turn to ashes and vanish by the wind. You mean I've been writing for the sake of an empty dream or a hallucination? You mean that I betrayed my own people? The Silent City? You know well that I sacrificed my life for them.

Night lurks beneath the sun. Stars blink as if they confide in each other a secret. I watch them. They collide. It sounds petrifying. Dark clouds appear out of this collision. Nature is taking revenge from itself. It is the first time in my life that I fear the night and the dark. I don't want to finish writing, and I feel that the last word will put an end to my life. Words, like termites, were biting my life and my age as they were doing my mission. I would have never thought of being afraid of demise this much.

Resho is watching his friend. He is still sleeping. Out of panic, Resho hugs him (me?) and then closes his notebook and his eyes as well. His body is so cold that he envies him for sleeping tremendously tranquil and comfortably numb inside the indifferent cardboard box. Death for Resho is the apex of adventure in that it removes human masks and grants soul all the strength of body to fly higher and lighter. The bodiless soul walks through time and place.

Rays of sunlight snake through the leafless branches and shine on those two creatures. The chilly morning wakes his friend up. As soon as he sees Resho's lifeless body, his scream tears apart the sky. Fear fills him so much that he escapes from even himself. He runs to inform the girl of Resho's death.

A whole lotta things in this story were like a fog for me, you feel me? I couldn't never wrap my head around it. And man, a death like that for a cat who put thousands on the map? That ain't right, not one bit. Tawuse Melek chose him, for real, put him on some mega mission. He was the only one who could speak for the folks history brushed aside. He always used to tell me, if a nation ditches its past, the future gonna come down on it hard.

I'll be real, I was always kinda scared to spill about his life. His detachment and being on his own, that stuff spooked me. Maybe just his girl and me, we was his main peeps who got him. Ever since I got tight with Resho, I've been having more talks with myself. Seeing him made me lose interest in university and churning out them articles. I wanted to stick to art, for real. Maybe that's why we clicked so tight.

He put me onto the smell of wet bricks, somehow. Got me searching for who I am, where I'm from, trying to wrap my head around what went down with me and my folks. I don't figure this story can hold it all, you know? I gotta dig deeper. This land's got a whole bunch more painful tales waiting to be told.

Resho used to open up to me 'bout everything, spillin' his memories, his dreams. He had this feelin' like he'd kick the bucket once he laid down his dreams 'bout Omar Kawar and Silent City. He told me to wrap up his mission so he could go out peaceful. He wanted to see the outcome of his hustle, not for fame or nothin'. He was dead set on givin' a voice to them burnt kids and forgotten souls, lettin' the world know.

I made up my mind, even if the university gave me the boot, I was gonna see this through. I was all in, so I gathered his writings 'bout his dreams, his memories, stitchin' 'em into a story. I'm hopin' I can bear this heavy load. While I was pullin' together them fragments and tossin' in a few extra bits, I always sensed someone in the mix. Sometimes that vibe would hand me the energy I needed to keep the words flowin', keep the spirit alive. On top of that, every mornin' when I'd rise up, I'd find some lines slipped in, stuff even Resho never put down. I can't figure how he pulled off them tricks. My one and only hope is to wrap up this tale and also come face-to-face with this bein' in the know, who's got it all down pat.

The Brothers of Time sing a hauntingly elegiac song over Resho's lifeless body. Their eyes fix upon the girl, now aged, carrying an empty canvas, as she draws near.

4

Since Resho chose to distance himself from society, the girl found herself submerged in solitude. What sent shivers down her spine was the fact that he had even forsaken his Room of Inspiration. How could he abandon his Cat? Her concern wasn't that Resho would find another companion in his loneliness, but rather that he might deprive the world of his paintings and writings. And so, for months, she bound herself to the canvas, painting a masterpiece to present to Resho— hoping that it might make him reconsider his decision of complete detachment

Sirwan did not know where her home was. He had the patience of Job to ask a lot of people, and finally he could find it. Amidst the heart of the city, there was an ancient locale, where narrow and dim alleyways intertwined, embracing a plethora of secrets within their embrace, and from which an eternal scent of earth perpetually emanated. Nestled in the midst of one such alleyway, stood a weathered, heavy wooden door, seamlessly integrated into the very fabric of the aged stone walls. He knew in his heart that this was the dwelling of the girl. With every step drawing him nearer, his heart beat faster, as though it sensed something yet concealed. An antiquated wooden light post adorned the scene, sporadically flickering and casting its enigmatic glow upon the surroundings.

I knocked, and she popped the door open real quick; it was like she'd been posted there, waiting for me or Resho. I stepped inside. My nerves were jangling so bad I was picking at my chest hair till it was like a bare wall. I had this twisted dream 'bout Resho, and I had to spill it to her, but I was at a loss for words; Resho was in a frenzy, hollering but couldn't snap out of it. He'd wrapped himself in a yellow blanket that turned into the canvas of his dreams. In the dream, I peeped

Resho, stone-cold under his oak tree, his body all decayed. Vultures and bugs gnawing on his remains. But what really got to me was termites chewin' on his notebooks, the ones he was jotting down the tales of Omar Kawar and Silent City in. His mission was fadin' away, disintegrating. Then I woke up, my skin's on fire. I knew I had to let her in on it.

Her whole room was splashed with acrylic splotches, and half-read books were lounging at every nook. Then I laid eyes on her painting, and I swear, I couldn't wrap my head around the fact that it was her own handiwork. That bubbly girl who used to be all about her crew had transformed into the loneliest soul on this planet. She'd aged a whole heap in the past few months. The signs were all over her face— wrinkles 'round her eyes, hair goin' gray. It was like her soul had grown in this grand way, and there wasn't a trace of that youthful naivety left in her.

She devoted her life to crafting this masterpiece, intending to resurrect Resho through it. Only pure art had the potential to rescue him from a mournful demise—art brimming with delicate imagination and imbued with the aroma of wet bricks. This could be the most profound gift of his existence. She aimed to plunge into the boundless ocean of meaning, where the fish of delicate fantasies would greet her. She understood the sacrifice this demanded, yet her yearning to revive Resho overpowered all else. Amidst unanimous circumstances that urged Resho to withdraw into the jungle as a recluse, the girl shared a final encounter with him. She proposed a rendezvous a year later, beneath the oak tree, grasping at the possibility of rekindling what they once shared.

Rain drops create an incongruous rhythm on the rooftop. She walks across and along her room with intense anxiety. After finishing the painting, she poured the remaining colors in the yard, and now she gazes at the rainbow that rain drops made from them. She observes herself in the scattered colors; from the core of the reddish colors, a fish springs forth that dances in the rain floatingly. It ascends using the rungs of dark blue drops, only to descend again.

She contemplates the stark reality that nothing remains within her

24

to bestow the gift of painting. She feels her artistic creativity has been doomed to decay within the completion of this piece. Helpless but thrilled, without makeup, she goes to another room and dresses up in black. In façade, she seems happy; but underneath the surface an unconscious disquiet is chewing the root of her being.

I wrestled with myself big time to keep that dream under wraps, but man, my concern for Resho was gnawing at me. Finally, I just let it all out, spilled every single detail of that dream. She locked eyes with me, and I swear, her heartbeat was loud enough to hear. Not a peep from her lips, and she jetted outta the place, clutching that painting in her hands. I was hollerin', but she didn't hear a lick, and my chest hair was gettin' the brunt of my fidgeting. I trailed behind her, but she got swallowed by the black of the rain. No clue what was gonna go down with her and that painting.

Dishevelled, pale, but beauteous and with an anxiety mingled with excitement, she heads toward Resho's oak tree which used to be their rendezvous. Never has she experienced fear and excitement simultaneously as such. Her body is saturated in the cruelty of the rain.

The raindrops apathetically knock on her canvas. The colors are bleeding, and Resho's portrait is being carved upon the streets, the pavements, and the walls of the city. A sublime fear, an understanding, a heavy burden of feeling what the victims had felt, fall down on the city with the raindrops. Resho has just passed away. People bring their Tamuras and Dafs. They stay under their balconies and, wholeheartedly play music. By playing Sar Tarz Maqam, they bid her farewell. The melodious sound of their instruments becomes the susurration of trees and mountains. The girl looks back and sheds tears for the unity of people, tears full of pride and honor. All the alleys and streets are saturated in the smell of wet bricks. She has never loved people this much.

She crosses the cemetery and arrives in the jungle, a place in front of Resho's inspirational room, under the high and stony mountains, and in the heart of the immortal oak trees where Resho passed away. Here and there, after the 16th of month of death, time and place have frozen forever and every one of the victims has been encapsulated in an untold tale, more that seventy thousand and twenty four tales . . .

The girl has aged, her delicate hands cradling a blank white canvas. She gazes upon two towering men, their beards thick and lengthy, their voices raised in a mournful dirge over Resho's lifeless body. It's her first encounter with the Brothers of Time. They sing the sorrowful melody of Mor, a song for the departed and the departing. She had previously only heard about them from Resho.

It is no longer raining. She stares at their eyes as if not with hers but with thousands of eyes. While she is listening to their song of sorrow, her eyes are getting bigger inside which there appear many other small ones. She gets mesmerized like the time Resho revealed his secret about his Room of Inspiration, the window and the Cat. She wants to approach them but they disappear. The spell is gone, and she gets her natural eyes back.

She leans her canvas to Resho's tree, kisses his lips, and starts digging the ground with her small fingers. The sun rises, and, with her bleeding fingers, she drags his body inside the grave. Hours has passed since he passed away yet he smells like wet bricks and his body seems fresh. She goes inside the grave, and lies on his body for hours. He smells like a newly-born baby. She comes out of the grave, fills it with oak tree leaves and branches, and puts her blank canvas on it as a gravestone.

Even his death is the continuation of his artistic career.

She finds Resho's notebook under the tree with a key on it. Resho has left the key of his house for his girl. She picks his writing notebook and places the key in her pocket. She looks around and observes the trees. The only dried tree is Resho's whose roots are growing to put Resho's body inside its arms, therefore he never dies there.

She feels the movement of the roots under her feet.

5

As soon as the Brothers of Time were born, the dead spirit of two hundred thousand and twenty four people, who were the victims of the Anfal genocide, blew into their body and soul. The twin brothers are the bitter fruits of the dispirited history. They never perish and time and place never make sense to them. After their birth, no one no more feared the cold death by the virtue of a halo of tranquillity that seized their city. Thereafter, the dead were buried with the sublime music of Daf and Tamura while reciting verses of Kalam, the sacred text of the Kurds. Nothing could exhilarate or sadden people, they knew the truth.

The Brothers of Time were aware of everything, and they knew the future of humanity, past and present. They were not confined in the prisonhouse of language and their songs had no words. When I heard their song, I felt the heaviness of an untold secret resided in the deep valley of history thousands of years old. No one chose a name for them but I dubbed them the Brothers of Time.

After their birth, people knew they will be put in mass graves or will be killed by chemical bombs soon, yet they admitted that, therefore they started forgiving each other, and kindness was the word of their tongue. They never talked about their death though they all knew it, and they were given the grace to create their own death.

After their birth, they aged twenty years within two weeks. Now they were young boys ready to obtain knowledge of all times. By getting to know everything, they became as old as their father, Omar Kawar, and they never aged more. Time froze in forty for them.

They were the sons of eternity and for this, Resho, a man of inspiration and spirituality, mattered a lot to them. The greatest concern of the brothers was the landlessness of those people died of the Anfal genocide. At nights, they searched for their consanguine brothers and sisters who were buried alive. They have been digging up the earth to find and put them inside their graves. They went to over four thousand villages which were eradicated on the map, and more than thirteen cities completely annihilated. They found more than two hundred thousand and twenty four people, laid them in their tombs, and planted an oak on each grave. This way, they could soothe their souls which were tainted with the ignorance of history. Resho did not know this aspect of their life; if he did, he would understand his dreams better.

Resho was unaware, but the Brothers of Time knew well that all those villages were ruined, and the entire populace was being coerced to migrate towards two distant cities, with the aim of augmenting their population. This stratagem was designed to facilitate the establishment of two governments in these cities, ensuring a smoother process. Their ulterior motive was to compel the people to forsake their ancestral lands, their way of life, and their cherished customs, ushering them into a new phase of existence that would be unnatural and more amenable to manipulation.

Currently, they maintain a solemn vow of silence, and during the nights, they gather beneath Resho's tree to mourn him. Since they began their singing there, Resho's tree has begun to blossom and unfurl leaves along its branches.

6

Nowhere quite like a graveyard can evoke such a sense of the supernatural. In the twilight hours, when the wind intertwines with the rustling of leaves and branches, and the mournful voices of the Brothers of Time blend, the essence of death flows effortlessly onto the bones, the flesh, and the spirits of humanity. In this place, as you tread its cramped pathways and contemplate the inscriptions on the gravestones, you find yourself envisioning your own name etched into the stone. Your contemplation of mortality rekindles, dispelling the illusion of immortality that may have lingered in your thoughts.

These issues immerse the girl in a sea of tranquillity, and lonely like before, on that same grave under the same oak tree, she can read Resho's notebook in a condition replete with mysticism of death. She wants to keep vigil to make the best use of time; she does not want to lose these moments of sublime feelings. Ever since she discovered the notebook, she refrained from unsealing it. However, under the moonlight that bathes the unmarked grave, an eerie depiction of an elderly man—an image Resho had described to her in the past—captures her gaze. At that time, she had trusted his words but couldn't truly grasp their essence. Now, the same sensation Resho had experienced courses through her. Determined to overcome her apprehension, she steps fearlessly into the realm of his words.

She bites her lips, and a drop of blood reddens the white canvas.

I don't know what he wants from me. Why did he want me to write? My career is to paint, and I feel that just colors can wash the colorlessness of my life away. Just colors can portray the mysteries of my life. I clearly feel the impotency of my words. He wants me to impregnate them with a mission. My fate is in his hands, and I can sense it. He determines my dreams, my writings, and I know this is not me who writes; this is him. I have seen Malak Taus, the Leaders of the Archangels, in my dreams. 'Leave the colors. Your mission will be accomplished by words only,' the last time he came, he murmured some words then went away.

From that time on, my hands are dead to touch of brushes and canvases. I desire to paint. I just can't. He sits on my mind, and so heavy weighs he that I get obliged to write to get my mind at ease and light again. However, I love this mandatory creation. Melek Tawus and I know that I am not good at writing. Maybe my mission is not letting the words surrender to negligence. Maybe I have to write in order to add to the warehouse of words in Kurdewari, the land of the great Kurdistan; so vast that it could emancipate the dead from the agony of oblivion. Perhaps my calling is to breathe life into a dead with every word I write.

I wasn't fond of continuing my education in painting since I believed that going to university to study art demolishes creativity. Someday, I went to a park near university to have some fresh air, and I saw an old man in white who caught my sight. I sat beside him on the bench. As soon as I sat there, he told me some words which sounded ambiguous. It sounded like a very ancient language. Like the language of the Kalam texts, it was abundant with the essence of unity. It brought before my eyes "from cow to fish" of the life of this land. By staring at his eyes, I saw all my life in a fleeting moment. A sublime fear blew into every cell of my body and soul. I can't forget the weight and grandeur of his look. I closed my eyes and when opened, he had vanished. Afterwards, my life was put on a spell. A magic so strange to words, colors, and notes. My dreams, fantasies, and thoughts were crowded with magically eccentric images. Thereafter, the children of Silent City and a man named Omar Kawar stepped into the threshold of my life.

I really have no idea what he chose me for this time. What did he find in this full of suffering life of mine that told me to write my life? He said that only words can put into the minds of people the sufferings of this nation. But, the more I know people, the more I understand that these people see images but don't read words; then how can they feel the sufferings, the agonies? Do they really want to feel them?

I don't know from where to start. I don't know when the page of my life has been turned. Maybe from the time Tawuse Melek came to my dreams, or the time my shabby girl came to my painting exhibition, or perhaps when I started writing my dreams and the narratives of Omar Kawar.

I have to translate picture to words. Surely, there is something hidden in words that they say, 'in the beginning was the Word, and the Word already existed."

She cannot read anymore. Resho's words have transfigured her eyes into a vortex full of images. She is drowned in the whirlwind of time. She observes all her life with Resho on the blank canvas. Her destiny has been determined to gaze and to behold. She sees his sufferings and gradually understands why he wanted to be alone in the jungle. She closes the notebook.

Since Resho went into a perpetual slumber under the oak tree, the girl's mind has been riled like a wrecked ship inside a tumultuous sea. There she sits by his grave ruminating over her deep relation with him at the Centre of Universe. They have been experiencing silence, night, and dream in there. She goes back to days whereby the only reason for Resho to stay inside society was to see her painting. She gave Resho a word to paint to the last breath, to devote her life and energy to be a wanderer in the beauteous world of colors, and to help him grow too. Resho was the one and only who gave her ideas, he was her unique confidant.

Her tears fall upon the white canvas on his grave. Trembling beneath the shelter of the oak tree, her hands pressed to her ears, she releases a scream that reverberates through the expanse of the jungle. The breath expelled from her mouth crystallizes, showering the trees and gravestones with a delicate frost, akin to glistening crystal. Her outcry disturbs the slumbering spirits of the departed, an unsettling disturbance. Restless, much like an orphaned child yearning for her mother, she aches for Resho.

She has dedicated herself to crafting a masterpiece intended for Resho. However, in the end, she believes it has all been in vain. Her wellspring of inspiration has run dry, and she feels the need to enter Resho's room—a place she was never permitted to enter. There, she hopes to reconnect with his essence, catch sight of his Cat, and gaze out the window to reignite her artistic spark. She perceives that her ability to paint has been forever lost, a torment that gnaws at her. In order to tap into Resho's fount of inspiration, she must venture into his room. Before that, though, she knows she must complete reading his notebook.

Never can I forget that relaxingly dark light: a relaxation full of pain of admitting. That night I admitted I was under surveillance of two all-knowing beholding eyes, the eyes of my Melek Tawus, my disobedient Archangel. From that night on, I have always awaited its finale. Despite knowing that its coming would burn all my being, it is impossible resisting it. So irresistible am I whenever I am facing him. When that light shone from no source, all my muscles and mental cells were tightened. I was haunted; I was occupied; I was made motionless. I experienced the most soothing, the most sublime, yet the most awe-inspiring moment of my life. That light was blended with the smell of wet bricks. It made clear the secret of that smell. A smell with which I was grown. It made me seek my identity, my language, my culture; things forgotten by people. Things that never make sense without land. It is the land that gives meaning to them. The land is like a mother that holds her baby in her arms. Now the baby is motherless, feeling alone and empty. Our mother is . . .

If I ever happen to be able to forget that night, I will never forget Sirwan's uncontrollable tears, and the moment he got goose bumps. This event has immortalized our bond. Afterwards, we understood each other more. Tawus found something in us that showed himself to both of us.

After resigning from university, Sirwan directly came over to enliven our memories at the Center of Universe; a room which is the center of universe for me. It is my scriptorium (these very words that you are reading now have been written here), my studying room, and my heaven for listening to music; a place that hosts my girl, Sirwan, and two hundred thousand and twenty four victims of genocide.

When I was a child, this room became my shelter. I used to accumulate some bricks and make them wet. The wettish smell of bricks would drive out fears that the black ghost behind the window, with fattish dark face, horrifying big eyes, and thick eye brows, had inserted in the depth of my vulnerable being.

I have been grown here; I have played Tamira here; I have read books here, I have dreamt, talked, and written about the Silent City, I have smelt the scent of her body here, and here is a place in which I have listened to many pieces of music. Listening to music here chains my mind to the movement of notes which results in experiencing moments of intense desire for escaping from this wintriey world.

Here I realized the depth and meaning of night and darkness, and here sheltered me from the burning and torturing sunlight. Roots of the oak tree in the yard have infiltrated my room through the stairs and corners of the roof, and drenched here with a sense of nature.

When I was a child, I dreaded my father. Of course, I am happy about it now. So deep was the fear that it has turned into a great source of inspiration for my writings. Furthermore, it caused this basement, which is the Center of Universe, to become a sanctuary for me now. I love my father. He was so cruel that made me grow independently which culminated in discovering this sacred place.

I loved snow fight at winters but my father didn't let me go out to play with my friends. A very cold night, I broke the ice, and he had my mother come and take me home. I was so afraid that I shaved my head and eyebrows clean; I thought he wouldn't recognize me that way. My brother came too and they were both pulling me on the ground. By force, they took me inside the yard. There, I could see his round black face and big eyes with his hand on the window. He was staring at my eyes, and all the fears of this world ate into my mind. I got speechless. I wish he tortured me physically. They closed the door, and I couldn't escape. I didn't go upstairs where my father was; instead, I went downstairs, into the basement.

That night was the beginning of the history of my seclusion. Bit by bit that night, I felt shadow and darkness. For the first time in my life, I lived in coldness. Back then, the Centre of Universe was a warehouse where extra heaters and other furniture were stuck there; I didn't care since I was alone with myself. The tranquillity of loneliness and gazing into darkness became my nocturnal and pleasurable habits; listening to the monologue of crickets mingled with the silence of night became the hobby of my life. The echo of music would inundate my mind with illusions without taking addictive drugs. My residence at the basement caused music to have the greatest role in my life. Gradually, music notes would turn into colors in my mind, and it became my most beautiful mental illness. The Peacock Angel, the God's deputy, descended and showed himself in the right place; he well knew the mesmerizing power of my room.

I adore my father. He has done me the most influential favor of my life. That intense fear led to immortalizing thousands of victims who have been helplessly massacred.

I have never let myself paint here; it is tainted by the presence of others. Many of my friends would come here to stay with me, and I couldn't paint in their presence. Before Tawuse Melek made me write, I would paint where, through the window, the howl of wind and high mountains had played with my soul, and where oak trees had strengthened my eyes. I would always paint in my Room of Inspiration and in presence of my Cat. I write Cat with capital C since it is the main character of my life, let alone this text. I have never taken my girl there. It is the only place that my true self is revealed, where the window opens then the Cat comes in.

My grandmother had given me that room before she passed away. It is located in the second floor where its window opens to high mountains, oak trees, and the graveyard.

However, the room in which I spent my childhood is a basement in an old house whose yard is shadowed by an enormous oak tree. My room is located underground, cool in summer and warm in winter. The yard is always cool due to the shadow of the oak, yet I wash the yard and pour water on its walls whose bricks are nakedly visible and also the tree. The coolness and smell of wet walls breeze into my room. That way I can write better since I get inspired; that is why I love summers.

Resho called his spot the Center of the Universe, and let me tell you, it was exactly that for me too. When I slid into his room, ain't no holdin' back. Real talk, I was straight up anticipating my next visit. He had these mirrors, each one sportin' a candle. And once that Tamira kicked up its tunes, everybody was locked in. That room, man, it swamped me in my own deep thoughts.

He used to write the narratives in this room, abovementioned by Sirwan, because of the mission Malik Taus, the god of Lalish, had given to him. Most of the chapters of this book were written there especially the ones about Omar Kawar. Every corner of his room could be inspirational for his writings. Before writing his dreams down, sometimes, he needed to prepare a stage for writing. He would turn off the lights and cover the door with a dark cloth; he would light some candles and play a highly melancholic song while watching the drawings he cranked out about the Silent City; every flame of the candles was dancing and pictures were flickering. In this way, the images of Omar Kawar and the Silent City would roam in his mind.

He was writing even at the moment just before he died. I wish he could pay more attention to the things that I had shown him whether in his dreams or when he was awake. I wanted him to fully understand what I meant by them. He did his best but it was not, it is not enough.

That night, we struck gold-- something that really flipped the script on my life. Sittin' there in front of a mirror, he had a long, dark, straight beard, and hair like shadowy pearl strings cascading down his sun-kissed shoulders. He was gettin' down with that Tamura. His head was bowed, those big multi-colored eyes of his were sealed shut, and his fingers on them strings were conjuring Riz strokes like you couldn't tell his hand from the bowl of the instrument. That instrument's fire could melt icebergs in the Arctic, and its melody could bring together four nations near a mighty river. It could transport a person back to when the world was ruled by nature. Don't believe me? Then ask me, man.

Listenin' to his Tamura that night, that burnin' sound was luggin' a history older than time itself. The notes, especially that Fa sharp, had this sort of mystery. I tried to break it down, but man, it was like chasin' smoke – just couldn't pin it down. Tryin' and failin', it set me ablaze, that feelin' of not gettin' to the core of that emptiness. Them Tamura notes was weavin' a story that never seemed to tie up, and I was just waitin' for the punchline. But it ain't take me nowhere. The more I chased, the hotter it got, you know? Huntin', burnin', spinnin' – I was caught in this cycle, like a spiralin' melody.

He'd be jammin' on that Tamura right there, and maybe that's why he dubbed his room the Center of the Universe.

There was a whole bunch of self-portraits on them walls. Surreal self-portraits where his whole vibe was mixin' up with them oak tree roots. 'Bout half of his art was all about himself, but each one had its own flavor. He was seein' himself in a new way in every single piece. He'd drop knowledge, say those joints were the Anfal victims, and the Brothers of Time planted them oak trees on their resting spots. As the trees grew, their bodies got all tangled up with them roots, like a deep connection growin' strong.

I peeped at my watch, it was almost daybreak. He cut the tunes, blocked that li'l gap under the door lettin' in the light, and sparked up more candles.

Resho dropped a line 'bout Tawuse Melek, but I couldn't wrap my head 'round it. Back in the day, I was all 'bout the bling and stuff. Me and Resho, we always had this vibe clash 'bout what art's all 'bout and his thoughts 'bout somethin' outta this world. Dude thought that creative juices flow from some unknown spot, but not from this world. He had this belief that artists get chosen by this vibe-filled bein' he called Malik Tawus.

When I got up on Resho, every now and then I'd catch a vibe of some metaphysical thing. My head would get all deep and tangled with somethin' I ain't know how to put into words, you feel me? But then came that night. Oh man, I ain't never gonna erase that night from my memory. It's stuck with me for life. That night, I peeped every single word of this book all at once, like a quick flash.

"I been feelin' like my mind be weighin' down for a while now.," I said. "I'm feelin' somethin' I can't put into words, you know?." I was shivering.

"I always feel and believe in the god of this land," Resho firmly replied.

"Shoot, I ain't even sure. Can't pick a name for that thing that's sittin' on my mind, ya dig?."

After moments of intense silence, suddenly, the candles were extinguished without any discernible cause, and an exceedingly potent, dark light commenced radiating upon the door, concealed beneath a black cloth. Every muscle in Sirwan's body tightened in reverence, and he found himself overcome by irresistible tears. Likewise, Resho's heartbeat reverberated as though it might burst from his chest, and his scream echoed with a faint, high-pitched resonance. The luminosity endured for a span of seven seconds, and just as abruptly as it had begun, the candles were rekindled.

As Sirwan and Resho locked their gazes, an unfathomable verity unfurled before them—a truth woven into the tapestry of their connection. Within the depths of each other's eyes, a spectral city materialized, its labyrinthine alleys and cobblestone streets teeming with a haunting congregation of the departed. These were no ordinary souls, but rather the remnants of forgotten narratives, lifeless words woven into the fabric of the city's existence.

The weight of this revelation settled upon them, a realization that they themselves were enshrouded within this spectral city, its essence threaded through their very beings. Yet, the knowledge they bore was not one of despair, but of destiny. An immense purpose coursed through their veins, a purpose akin to the giants of ancient myths.

For they understood that their existence was tethered to a colossal mission—one that transcended the boundaries of mortality itself. They were endowed with the power of words, a gift to animate the lifeless, to transform the silence of death into the symphony of existence. In this city of the departed, Sirwan and Resho were chosen, not as mere inhabitants, but as the architects of resurrection, breathing vitality into the slain stories that lay dormant in the alleys of silence and oblivion.

7

Repetitious dreams have flooded Resho's mind with chaotic and appalling images since Tawuse Melek, the god of colors, walked inside his life. This divine encounter has triggered a profound transformation within him. These dreams held significance beyond mere chance; he sensed that he was destined to achieve something, leading him to perceive the dreams as serendipitous. He attempted, numerous times, to piece together the symbols and decipher their meaning without mentioning them to anyone. He saw in the dream that that he was rolling his life down like a gargantuan stone from top of a mountain at the middle of which he got awakened by knocks on the door.

The girl arrived to visit him, and as she reached for the door knob, she noticed it was adorned with two intricately carved stone snakes, a sight she had never encountered before. His face revealed his unease, a clear indication that a nightmarish experience had left his mind in disarray. To prevent descending into madness, it was imperative for him to put down the details of this encounter in writing.

The wind howl and the symphony of tree branches are mingled with the grunting of pigs. The coughing sound of artilleries and tanks beyond the mountain has synchronized the rhythm of my heart with that of volleys that have turned the river into a pool of blood. The bombers discharge flammable and chemical gasses on people, and I, inside the jungle, can observe them all. Numerous hissing snakes have hung themselves from the branches of the thick woods. My head is positioned a bit lower than theirs, exactly three centimeters of distance. Out of the blue, they misconstrue me for a tree and start crawling down and twisting around my body. I am tightly-sealed tied, and I can hear nothing but hissing. Hard and rarely can I breathe.

An old woman in black, whose long hair drags the dried branches and leaves behind her, can be seen from afar who is approaching me. I think that she bears a remarkable resemblance to my girl. She has big staring eyes with an absorbing power of observation. Thousands of other small eyes seem to have been located inside her light blue eyes. I can see their flickering lights. I feel that she bears the heaviness of many thousand eyes of children who have insouciantly chosen her eyes as a place to settle. Her eyes are screaming with tears. I see all my life in her eyes; a blank canvas, Tawus, my two rooms, burnt children, two brothers, my tree, and many other things that I feel will happen to me. I can feel them with every inch of my body and soul.

Suddenly, many couples of bright eyes appear under the oak trees. All the jungle flickers. They crave for something. They want something. They don't talk. They have lost their speech. I do too. The faces get visible. I can't look at their scalded faces, burnt hair, and swelled lips. I scream with no voice. All that can be heard is the hissing. Then, I close my eyes. The snakes creep down my body, and the old woman turns her back on me receding and fading out in darkness. Thereafter, I observe a man under an oak tree writing while gazing at a white canvas. Two men with the same height and shape are going toward a theatre.

After this dream's repetition over a period of time, bit by bit, Omar Kawar and the Silent City penetrated inside his life and his dreams.

Somewhere in this world, somewhere in placelessness, I can see thousands of children being burnt all at once and, everyone in one place, maybe in a bleeding Sunday, being liquidated. They have sneaked into my dreams, and I know there is no coincidence at work regarding these people and me. They are forgotten and forgetfulness is the most terribly irremediable pain. I am well aware that reviving them is painfully laborious since I have a very vague image of them. An idea hit my mind, and I am going to paint it even if its heavy burden annihilates the delicate seeds of my fantasy; I will paint them even if Tawus, the god of my land, doesn't let me. I will entitle it The Children of Silent City. As soon as I close my eyes, they all appear before my sight. Their swelled lips and burnt faces set my mind on fire. I am awaiting the melting of my brain at any time. I crave to echo their voice inside the tiny and dark alleys of history. Even if the world remains unaware of them, even if people close their eyes to them, as long as I alone know what troubles them, perhaps I can bring them some happiness. They all must be from one country (mine). I realized this by their similar faces, and I just look forward to some signs to discover their identity, then I will find out the reason of their sad demise.

I am in urgent need of looking at my inspirational Cat's eyes. In the depth of its eyes, I can observe the children's being flamed inside the jungle. I understand this by the agony in their looks.

When he wrapped up his masterpiece, I hollered at him, "Can I slide over to your spot?" But nah, he wasn't having it. Instead, he brought the artwork to my crib. It was on a black backdrop, and right in the center, them milky skeletons were all twisted up like tree branches. Their eye sockets were big enough to catch attention, and the empty spaces around their eyes, noses, and mouths were rocking a cool light blue. It looked like fire flames, you know?

8

Omar Kawar: The First Narrative

The girl, little by little, understands Resho's detachment and believes in his great soul which was chosen by the god of languages and the children of Silent City. Now, she is assured that it was only Resho's great soul that could give home to thousands of burnt children. Resho sacrificed himself for immortalizing those whose voices have been lost and suffocated in the black, cold, and full-of-steel tunnel of history. He was aware that a whole nation's everlasting relief depended on his pen.

He was the voice of the unvoiced; he belonged to no one but everyone. This is happening while he remains mostly unaware of the secret; he does not know why the cata-death-strophe occurred in the silent city. Furthermore, he is unaware that the image of Omar Kawar and his son is not an accurate representation of what actually happened, as the photographers orchestrated the scene to serve their own interests. If I were to reveal the entire truth to him all at once, undoubtedly his mind would implode, and his soul would be tainted. I should guide him to understand it gradually, bit by bit and very slowly

These dreams have so obliged me to write that not writing them revitalizes a sense of treachery in my shelterless self. Betraying to the collective soul of a nation whose people, whose burnt people, have been forgotten in the mind of people. I can't stand the world's oblivion.

I try to link these sets of sequential dreams with the ones repeated before, and I feel I am about to get somewhere sooner or later. The previous ones were fixed yet repetitious; however, these ones are impregnated with a narrative line. They rile my soul; however, my passion for seeing them doesn't decay.

I wander in a room with red walls and big windows. Behind each window, some

children are impatiently waiting. In a corner of the room, a midwife in Kurdish clothes stands beside a woman who is about to give birth to her child. She is called Samie. Her stomach is getting bigger and bigger. A man walks inside, and the midwife calls him Omar Kawar. He is Samie's husband. Anxiously, he caresses her hands. After a while, a boy, around seven, comes in. Omar Kawar summons his son, Mohammad Shwan, over to stay beside his mom.

Samie's stomach is swelling. In a fleeting moment, her children are born. Pink blood and plasma spurt out of her stomach so much that they color most of the walls and the roof as well. Pink blood flows through the streams of the city and beneath the trees. Pink snows are falling on the city and its surrounding oak jungle. Her seven beautiful daughters, one by one, are opening their eyes to this world while Samie gives me a full-of-sorrow smile. She feels no pain. The hairless children behind the windows are calling out the birth of the seven sisters' news to the city.

As soon as they were born, the sisters started giggling. They giggle so loudly that a wave of happiness dominates the entire city. "It was the laughing that didn't let her die," The midwife later said she has been tittering so much that all her stomach muscles have been contracted; therefore, for a while, she won't be able to sleep in comfort.

Omar Kawar invites all people of the city to the oak jungle to name his daughters. Young men and women play Daf and Tamura. The elderly people are taking off their clothes then come to the middle of the crowd. Turning around, dancing, and moving their heads up and down with their long hairs hanging in the air, they sing a song in choir:

> *Graveyard was a place*
> *In which I was born*
> *Oak was my Mom*
> *Daddy was cold stone*

> *Ask the moon and stars at night*
> *Ask the sun that shines ill-light*
> *And the dark that holds me tight*

I never lose grip on this life

Oh city of hope and dread
Full of love and bloodshed

The melody of Tamura is me
Creator of death is me
Mountains grow out of me
Borders are washed away by me

Oh city of hope and dread
Full of love and bloodshed

Omar Kawar puts his seven daughters on a big branch of a tree, but doesn't declare their names. Something in an evanescent glimpse crossed his mind to leave them nameless. They all look alike.

The day after, Omar Kawar comes back from theatre rehearsal with Mohammad Shwan. Hand in hand, they happily arrive home. He confuses his seven daughters. Goes near and smells them, touches them, and now he can differentiate his children.

They are grown now. On a land covered in snow, they are planting wheat. Their faces are changing, and, gradually, their similar appearances are getting different. They are having lunch, and Omar Kawar can easily distinguish his children. He is dancing, and the earth shudders. The seven sisters still grant smiles and happiness to the city.

As a ritual, at weekends, all people, from kids to octogenarians, go on their rooftops to play music and dance. Old women and men surrender their long hairs to wind. Their hair locks are dancing in wind like a sparrow in the gale. They ring around each other on rooftops and Dhikr. The rhythms of Daf and the soothing *melodies of Tambur melt their minds in their bodies.*

Suddenly, the scene changes to under a dried oak tree where Omar Kawar is reading his writings to Mohammad Shwan, but only his lips are moving.

I saw them live in my dreams. If I were as sprightly and full of life as they were, I would paint more, play Tamira more, and write more. These people are themselves the truth of life, the result of the bond between art and nature. They didn't want others to dominate their motherland since they smelled the wet bricks.

Instantaneously, the sky gets black. Many bombers are flying above the city. Children hide their instruments; women hug their husbands; husbands smell their wives' hairs. Tanks and soldiers surround the city. Gunners are descend the mountains, and the blackness of their military gowns blackens the white snows. The bombs are dropped, and bricks are broken down like glasses. Children wet the broken walls with water in small broken kegs to smell the wettish bricks.

Ssssshblammmmmmmmm . . .

Omar Kawar's first son, Mohammad Shwan, fell on the ground. He went on the rooftop to play Tanbur, and the bang of the bombs dropped him down. His brain splashed over the ground. The seven sisters rushed out of their house and wrapped their brother in a pink cloth. All men and women of their city dressed in black and followed them to the graveyard with curved Dafs whose rings were dropped and whose grease got dried; Tamuras with cracked bowls and twisted necks that sounded disaster yet sent shiver on the earth.

Two men who seemed to be brothers went under my oak tree and sang an elegy.

The sisters unearthed the ground and put Mohammad Shwan in it. They recited verses from Kalam, their holy book, and returned home. I was there on his marooned grave. A typhoon blew and sepulchered me in the dust. A thickly dense shadow dragged me inside the tomb. My face was just one or two centimeters away from his eyes. He opened his eyes and started screaming. He came back to life, I could feel his breaths.

Mohammad's mother didn't attend the burial. She was expecting her twin sons and her stomach was already swelling up as if thousands of snakes had stung it. When Omar Kawar and his seven daughters arrived home, they saw one of the babies was born, and the second one was about to. Samie was dying while an aura of relief in form of oak tree's yellow leaves were pouring on the rooftop and raining on the windows.

9

Choppin' it up with Resho was straight-up mind-blowing for me. We vibin' to the tunes, chattin' 'bout all kinds of stuff: our art, his words, the visions he had 'bout Omar Kawar and that Silent City, and my future moves. But one thing he never spoke on was his girl. I ain't never caught wind of her name 'cause Resho, he ain't never let it slip. (Or maybe that's my own guilt, 'cause I ain't never picked a name for her.). He believed she was delicate, like one false word could shatter her to bits.

Resho bounced on me, left me hanging, all on my lonesome; he dipped on everything. After that twist in the road, I straight-up dipped out on education too and decided to pen a novel. I aimed to spin a tale 'bout Resho, his lady, and all them dreams he spilled to me. The real truth? Resho's the storyteller, the main scribe; I'm just piecing together the fragments of his life.

Oh, and by the by, I had a copy of them dream scribbles he penned. He handed it to me before he passed away. Only issue I had was that girl. She's a cornerstone in this narrative, but damn, I ain't know her well enough to weave her story. I only laid eyes on her once, and she barely dropped a word.

I had to step up and have a convo with her. She could've had a real big piece in this tale. I headed into the wilds, you know, the jungle. It wasn't exactly freezing, but I was shakin' nonetheless. As I got closer, the brothers' enchanting voices caught my ear. It was like I was hearing death itself, yet it was like a balm for my soul. Resho had always rapped 'bout their voices, but I ain't never heard it up close like that. After Resho dipped, they stuck 'round with the girl. They were jammin' on the Tembur, singin' the Khamushi Meqam:

Sip Resho, Resho do sip,

A venom this is, destiny's script.

Roar and fervor, they've had their play,

Your name 'Silent' I now overlay.

Their voices carried a mystical kind of charm, no doubt, but here's the twist... I was all kinds of mixed up. Resho had laid it out for me, said those brothers never let a word slip from their lips.

I strolled up closer to Resho's tree, and their voices started to slip like smoke on the breeze. That girl, she was deep into some Omar Kawar words. I arrived late to the party, a missed chance. Man, I wished I could catch her flow from the very start.

Omar chose no name for them.

In the dream, I felt it was me screaming inside the grave. I was about to be suffocated. I could feel my being buried alive with every cell of my soul and body, and I could inform no one. When I got awakened, a cold sweat wetted all my body; a coldness like that of death.

Mohammad Shwan was the first child who ascended into the land of children of Silent City, and Omar Kawar was the only father who later on witnessed all his children's death.

She sealed up Resho's draft, gripped it tight. Lifted her head, moonlight paintin' her face all clear. All of a sudden, she looked like she'd lived a thousand and one years. Did I bring that weight upon her? It was plain to see, she was carryin' a world of worry. I couldn't muster the guts to spill what went down on her. Stepped up, got closer, right by her side. Peeped her empty canvas. Hit me deep, like a ton of bricks. All her hustle gone like wind's blowin' it away. I was down in the dumps for her double loss—Resho six feet under, her art on the same grave.

Words got stuck in my throat for a hot minute. Gestured for her to open up, talk to me. Told her how I poured my soul into makin' Resho and her live on, fulfill his callin'. Said I was here to lend a hand, be of service, but I had to get to know both of 'em. She just listened, eyes not meetin' mine, lips locked. Not a single word to my questions.

I felt her, gave her space to be quiet. Her gaze stayed glued to that canvas, her spirit caught in the whirlwind of sorrow, rocked by Resho's leavin' like a thunderclap.

I'm sittin' here wonderin' why she feels so damn real. And why Resho, he feels like he's right next to me, like we tight. It's wild, I never thought I could leave behind these dreams of mine.

10

While studying painting in another city, he rented a house on the southern side of the city. He had difficulty getting along with the other students at the dormitory. He detested living with four others, each with their own distinct worldviews – like four rivers that never converge into one sea. He stayed there for only a month, yet its destructive effects haunted him for a long time. It left a scar on his soul, shattering his sense of loneliness. He couldn't even bring himself to play Tamura. It took several months until he could piece together his shattered fragments.

Dude couldn't quite keep the ends from fraying, had to snag this little, budget room down in the South, real near them train tracks. To be real, it was cramped, like a shoebox tight. I really wish I could've thrown him a bone. He was pretty good on the emotional front, didn't need too much proppin' up. But damn, I just wanted to be able to toss him some cash to ease the load a bit.

Man, he was keepin' it bare-bones. That room had just a light and four walls, that's it. Resho, he rolled in with his Tamira, a blanket, a pillow, and his painting, his trusty sidekick. Hung that painting and the Tanbur on the wall – two things that were right there with him day in, day out, until he kicked the bucket.

Resho yearned for someone with no speech ability; he believed that words often erode emotions. He longed for someone who deserved his silence. No one could truly fulfil his craving for solitude, so he remained immersed in his own mental realm. This introversion eventually found expression in a painting that encapsulated his loneliness. He reached a point where he no longer yearned for a person made of flesh and bone. Resho's connection with the painting predated his acquaintance with the girl.

The painting depicts a girl with eyes heavy with sorrow, her gaze fixed on distant realms of nostalgia that the modern beauty surrounding her fails to reach. A cigarette, an empty wine bottle, and a tipped-over glass are carefully placed on a desk beside her. Her right hand rests beneath her chin, while her left hand supports her other wrist, as if to anchor her unending contemplation. What torments her? Into which obscure annals of history does she gaze? Why does she resist returning to life's embrace? Why do the red hue of the wall, the brown of the chair, and the blue of the table fail to evoke any excitement within her? Why does her window open to a void? Even Resho himself lacked the answers. The girl occupies a chair with a wedding gown suspended from the ceiling behind her, and a curtain beside her that conceals an enigmatic space beyond.

Ever since Resho painted it, the figure's hair has been steadily growing, and now, after several years, it has become so long that it cascades down to the floor. Only a few brown spots remain visible; it's as though the figure has been brought back to life, existing amidst the vibrant colors while still trapped within her contemplation.

Back then, Resho was infected by the inertia and the routine of his room. Being lonely, listening to the same pieces of death-dealing music, looking at the same objects, smoking the same cigarette, and gazing at the same eyes of the same figure in the painting have isolated and ostracized his spirit the revival of which seemed far-fetched.

His one and only friend in that drowned-in-loneliness city was the girl in the painting, his patient stone. He confided his pains in a girl who was frozen in his colors. At nights, he was thinking if the girl could take on flesh and come to life, what would she ask him? He was thinking that if she brought her opinions with her, he would become all ears to listen to her silence, and let the music of her thought murmur between them.

I always looked at that girl in the painting with a little envy, you know? I always wished Resho could lean on me like a (real) friend; I think he did, but I always hungered for more of Resho 'cause he was my whole inspiration.

11

Omar Kawar: The Second Narrative

It is a while that Mohammad Shwan has died. I see Omar Kawar awakened; terribly sweating. Then, he twitchily looks for his pen and paper. Thinking about where to go, he hurriedly goes beneath my tree, and while gazing at the blank canvas, he starts writing. He keeps fidgeting with his pen. His writing turns out to be a handful of scribbled lines. He cries, and then he kisses the grave under the canvas. Out of the blue, I see the Brothers of Time carrying some paintings and taking them to the city theatre.

Omar Kawar passes the jungle then hikes the mount. After a while, he reaches the summit and sits there. Gazing at the sun which hurts his eyes, he picks a stone and throws it toward the sun. It is getting dark, and the stars bit by bit and one by one appear. He, out of relief, breathes softly and deeply. He stands up and sets off toward his oak tree. Beneath his tree are some empty gunnies and sacks along with some shovels. The echo of his shouting his son's name resonates down the valley. He picks a gunny and fills it with his sorrows. They pour out like dense liquid from his left ear and then get dried like stone. He picks a shovel and digs the ground some meters away from the tree and buries his sorrows.

Yellow are the tree leaves now that is the beginning of spring. After Mohammad Shwan's death, leaves have been yellow and brown in all seasons.

Omar has gone into a deep slumber on a big branch of his tree. When awakened, he beholds all the mountain is conquered by fog. He gets down the tree to go back to his city. So thick is the fog that he gets forced to pull aside layers of dense fog to get through. I am walking right behind him. When he approaches the city, he notices a not-so-deep well that wasn't there before. He turns back and stares at me. His lips are trembling and his look is very sharp. I can see in his eyes how distressed and stressed he is. He wants me to help him but I really can't. He doesn't know I'm just an observer.

He suddenly gets thirsty. I think he wants to drink water from the well. I am away from him just for half a meter. Craving for a handful of water, he looks down there. He pulls his head out immediately. Gets a gander again and a petrifying tumult is heard from the bottom of the well. It tosses his head out. It is the scream of thousands of kids. He is helplessly looking at me. The tears in his eyes are shaking down his trembling cheeks.

He sees the future in its most nude form. He looks down again and sees his burnt city. I can see everything. He sees people whose dead bodies are piled up upon each other; the displaced people are running toward mountains; children who are being smashed under people's feet; and old men and women whose lame legs are unable to run. The chemical bombs are affecting people. Everyone coughes and vomits a pink liquid. The sonic boom of bombers deafens people's ears; bullets and chemical bombs fall on people and the city but nauseatingly slow; the windows are being broken, and the gasses penetrate inside the houses of his fellow-citizens; children's eyes are getting bigger and bigger as they are more infected by the gases; and scalds disperse on their faces. He sees the entire city from a vantage point. The skin of his city is shooting blisters and scalds.

He sees mothers throwing away their children, he sees fathers who trample their own kids underfoot. Thousands of people are running in fear and hundreds of old and young people are smashed under their feet. No one knows about another one. No one feels the pains and fears of another one. No one sees another. It is the doomsday and parents do not recognise their own children. Neither do the children. Thousands of people who lost their homes are running towards the mountains. Thousands of others reach the immediate border to take shelter in another country. He sees their doomed destinies too. There, their children are stolen and their days and nights are spent by thirst and hunger while craving to return to their looted motherland. There, they become other people. They forget themselves. Their behaviours undergo deep changes.

Scenes are passing before his eyes, each one more burning than the other. The drops of water are shedding tears. He wants to pour water on the burnt-stricken hearts. It doesn't suffice; even the 'Sirwan' and 'Alwan' rivers . . . Ocean is indeed needed.

He is screaming for help yet no one hears him. He has lost his speech and voice. He sees his nine children in a glimpse. Their faces are glued to each other and all are burning together. The sizzling sound of their skins sets his mind on the symphony of uneasy blazes. He beholds his own lifeless body lying in the alley. From another country, some people arrive, fully equipped with masks and vials, swiftly making their way to the Silent City like vultures. They have been waiting for the chemical bombardment for a while. Cameras in hand, they capture artistic photographs of the city's dead and burnt bodies, intending to invoke fear in the hearts of their own countrymen with the harrowing images of the people in this desolate city.

They bring forth the lifeless body of Omar Kawar, and also his son, who lost his life at home. They place the son in his father's embrace. Omar Kawar's turban is not on his head. They bring another dead man's turban and place it upon his head. The cameras are turned on. They take a few steps back and . . . the shutter clicks . . . clicks . . . clicks . . .

He drops himself down the well, and I am abruptly awakened.

All my body was saturated in sweat. I went to the alley. I saw a dream so real that I felt I was walking at the bottom of the well.

The explosion of internal veins of my imagination

Turned the room into red.

The blood of my fantasy flew over the floor.

I could see the words of my mind shattering and tattering;

I opened the window

The alphabet of my mind sterilized every single soil,

Every tree grew leafless,

All the mountains blew apart,

They metamorphosed the earth into a hollow void,

The void of nothingness.

The girl closes the notebook. She thinks about the day that she can go to Resho's room to be exposed to his inspirations. She would smell the bricks of his room's wall from which Resho detached its plasters to pour water on them. He loved the smell of wet bricks.

She opens the notebook again.

12

Now that I'm writing, I keep telling myself I wish I never had that exhibition. This very event caused our familiarity. She was the only one who pondered on my works, and, nearly, her understanding of the paintings was what I had in mind. How could she read my mind? Those paintings were my mental ejaculations, and she analysed them so correctly that seemed like she has been taking a sojourn of many years in my mind. Who could imagine that?

Tawuse Melek has instilled in me many times, in my dreams and in real life as well, to have an exhibition. Like a child, it would come and sit on my mind so uncaringly. When I was a student and rented a small room in the southern part of the city, I confronted a little girl who was the embodiment of Tawus, and she directly commanded me to go back to my own city and hold my own exhibition. Then she vanished. I didn't know what to do. Like a bird in a howling gale, I couldn't choose my direction. Irresistible were his orders; many times her orders. Some other times it got incarnated in the flesh of an old woman; I have seen it in trees, in clouds, in children, in my Tanbur, and in my Cat. I am getting sure that it even determines my melodies. But I love to be like that stranded bird in a strong gale. Going with the flow with no specific destination is the apex of life for me.

I was chillin' at the crib when Resho came knockin' on the door. Dude never gave me a heads-up 'fore he rolled through. I kinda dig his spontaneous moves though. He hit me with, "A true friend surprises you with visits." It ain't like he was testin' me or anything like that; our bond didn't have no limits 'cause he was a part of me, a piece of my dream. Did he peep the fact I'm livin' in dreams? Maybe he just forgot givin' me the heads-up, 'cause he could be forgetful like that. Or maybe he felt so tight with me, he didn't feel the need to give me a heads-up. He stepped in and dropped some talk 'bout an exhibition. He was messin' with his chest hair so much it went bald, like a wall stripped of plaster.

He told me that Tawuse Melek had been pushin' him to put on an exhibition. Dude was complainin' 'bout losing his grip on decision-makin'. He figured he couldn't call all the shots. "It's like a hidden blessing, man. Showin' your stuff to folks would be real cool," I told him.

His left eye got all teary, and he just dipped without sayin' a word. Still ain't figured out why that left eye of his always got misty.

I ain't got a clue 'bout what Resho's talkin' 'bout with this god of Inspiration he mentions, but I do reckon any true artist with a real passion's got their own sort of personal vibe. Me, I call it inspiration, somethin' not everyone's got in their pocket. It's like we need these kinds of vibes, these Tawus, to make our art genuine. That inspiration, or what Resho calls Malik Taus, that's what brings out the true essence of your art.

The exhibition was not my idea at all; it was the Tawuse Melek's. I think it didn't know that being unknown and wandering in dark tunnel leading to no light and anonymity in the circle of the world are my utmost pleasures which are, for me, indescribable. I didn't want to be a celebrity. All I wanted was to adhere to my loneliness. I wish I didn't see her. Feeling different made me happy and that exhibition took it from me. There was another one like me with the same mindset. Realizing this fact shattered my illusion. I got disabused.

Every cloud has a silver lining though. She turned out to be mingling me more in my loneliness; therefore, I could do my mission.

We bore a remarkable resemblance to each other, mentally lonely, secluded, and saturated in art. Every inch of her body was impregnated with beauty of art. Every inch of her body fluctuated among Do, Re, Mi, Fa, So, La, Si. I knew it when I was playing Tamira.

There exists a void in our mind that gets enlarged day by day, and like a black hole, drags happiness and hope inside itself. She well understood this void of mine. I felt an immense void in her eyes too. There are some people that not only don't spoil your silence and loneliness, but they make you lonelier and deepen your silence. My girl was one of them.

I could feel she was walking on a sharp and tiny edge likely to fall down on the sublime land of art and be polluted in pain. She said I had changed her life, as if being mesmerized. Her eyes substantiated her words. I could clearly recognize her honesty out of the threshold of her eyes; they were full of mystery, spirituality, meaning and knowledge—a knowledge leading to difference and detachment. Knowledge causes not happiness, and it is sprung from the heart of darkness.

The angels are innocent and they lack the pleasure of knowledge. Eden is a place deprived of knowledge; knowledge means hell, means difference, and means introversion since it is involved in truth — a truth which is burning and its smoke blackens your innocence. It is a pain that affected the Brothers of Time in its cruellest. Anyone who has seen them, in person or in dream, is infected by this sublime pain.

I felt her face is a big eye full of small eyes. This made me unable to stare at her eyes.

Everything initiated from that sentence. Why did she ask me about my inspirations? She didn't know that my Cat could be a scar on anyone's mind. That sentence ended up in an ocean of fire. I don't know what was flaunting in my mind when those words were pouring on my tongue that way—maybe cruel, maybe soothing, maybe soft, I have no idea. If I knew, I would find a solution for the darkness that devours every bit of me.

I have been asked by many people many times but I evaded them. This time, I had the gut to unmask my secret. To be honest, it was burning me. It was clear she was not like them. It was clear she understood me, and she wouldn't ridicule me. How on earth could I guess I would lead her life inside the darkness in which I lived, and this event would become her turning point? Is darkness an evil thing? Is sadness . . . . Everyone should be entangled with the sadness of the children of Silent City.

She was the only one who realized my most sacred secret and who got aware of my source of inspiration.

She stops reading and gently closes the memory notebook. Enveloped in a trance, she succumbs to the haunting melody of the Brothers of Time, their Tembûrs resonating and undulating through the entire cemetery like waves. As she gazes at the grave, she reflects that even though his body rests beneath the ground, his words breathe life into all they shared, right before her eyes. Time can encapsulate an entire lifetime in an instant; yet, to truly sense and touch a person, a physical place is indeed essential. Space and place possess hearts as solid as stone. They've never truly aligned with time; if they had, anguish and restlessness would lose their meaning.

In the dim-lit cemetery, she strikes a match and draws the flame to the tip of another cigarette, as if invoking a portal through time. With a longing gaze, she imagines herself astride the ethereal waves of memory, riding the azure currents, all the way back to that enchanting juncture when their lives first converged within the walls of the exhibition hall.

13

The attendance of the girl at the exhibition was so unexpected.

In order to fit in with the other guests at her friend's party, she decided to go to the bazaar to find an appropriate dress. The guests included people who had just purchased their first samovar in the city, individuals who had sacrificed goats to celebrate their acquisition of an automatic iron, those sipping organic juice for the very first time, and others who possessed the determination to attend a monument dedicated to the peeling away of emotions However, she found herself at a book exhibition instead. Her eyes were insatiable in their desire to peruse the displays, hungrily investigating the covers. Oddly, no one seemed to be making any purchases. A thought crossed her mind: if the writers themselves bought fifteen volumes of their own books, perhaps their works would make it onto the list of bestsellers.

Amidst the various titles, she spotted a book with no mention of the writer's name on the cover. Its title was intriguing: The Smell of Wet Bricks. After a quick purse check, she decided to forsake the dress and happily purchased the book. As she held the book, she reached the end of the hallway where a set of spiral stairs beckoned. A sign caught her attention: "Painting Exhibition." With a sense of urgency and excitement, she ascended the stairs, quickly covering two floors.

Her hair, a bit disheveled, spilled over her face from beneath her scarf. Despite this, her large eyes and vibrant red lips bestowed a unique innocence and beauty upon her visage. Her youthful appearance often led others to not take her seriously; her baby-faced countenance seemed to overshadow her true potential. It was only Resho who eventually unearthed the hidden grandeur within her.

Resho positioned a colossal frame at the entrance of the exhibition, creating a portal through which the entire display could be viewed. Passing through the frame, she approached the first painting titled "The Opening Night of the Exhibition." Within the painting, numerous wanderers gazed at their surroundings, their eyes searching the empty walls. These figures possessed human bodies yet sported the heads of cows, sheep, and donkeys. Having studied the painting intently, the girl gently brushed her hand against her own face, a gesture that erupted into laughter, the sound reverberating throughout the exhibition space. Resho's attention was drawn to her, noting that she was the sole individual laughing, the only one grasping the underlying irony.

The subsequent painting depicted the isolation of a figure whose path diverges sharply from the crowd. This artwork portrayed a scene of soccer players, expending all their effort in pursuit of a football. Above them loomed a thick, black cloud. The spherical white ball, gleefully basking in the spotlight, rolled far away from their reach. On the contrary, on the other side of the canvas, a solitary figure paid no heed to their absurd endeavors. Lost in thought, he envisioned himself as a fish, adorned with vibrant scales. A man with a fish's head, his body draped in delicate droplets of imagination, he navigated the boundless journey of contemplation, meaning, and beauty.

The girl pondered if this figure could be the painter himself, and she interpreted the piece as a portrayal of his detachment from society—an artist who both comprehends and suffers. Those who possess greater awareness, she mused, become more vulnerable to the hostility of others. Seekers of knowledge are akin to fortune's soldiers, lacking an armor that leaves them vulnerable, like glass shattering upon exposure to the truth. As a result, they retreat from the cacophony and discord of those who evade imagination, individuals oblivious to their own circumstances. In both the figure depicted in the painting and Resho, there arose a protest and rebellion, armed with the sole weapon of isolation.

Resho's paintbrush seemed to gravitate toward detachment

without conscious intent. The girl's assumption proved accurate. Resho, removed from the bustling scene and positioned beyond the frame, was engrossed in the act of smoking a cigarette—his identification was effortless. With careful steps, she approached him, and he, sensing her purpose, rose to his feet. As they exchanged handshakes, the first deep and non-lingual relation occurred between them. In his grasp, her hand found a sanctuary as if he had known her for years.

Without hesitation, the girl inquired about the origins of his inspiration.

A shiver coursed down his spine. Answering this seemingly simple question felt like unveiling the sacred secret of his existence. He held the conviction that language was akin to fragile glass, poised to shatter at any moment, and the resulting glimmers of fracture had the power to ensnare minds in illusions. However, this instance held a gravity beyond the fragility of glass-like language. His response had the potential to unveil a truth capable of fracturing her own glass-like existence. While he could trust her, an undercurrent of fear still held him back, a fear of vulnerability to potential ridicule. Doubt and dilemma loomed over him like the cataclysmic clash of good and evil at Armageddon.

"There is a window in my room with a view over the sublime mountains that eyes can't fully behold them. There are oak trees on the hill foot and, when wind shakes them, their howl mingles with the voice of two legendary brothers at the heart of the woods. When I hear their voice, I feel a person lying down in a grave, as if being revived, beneath an oak tree at the bottom of a high mountain; there is a girl under the oak tree whose eyes are visible when I look at the oak jungle. I can't hear her but her look is so weighty. The dead body sings like a person who wants to tell a truth, but nobody understands his language. When I hear these voices and see that view, my mind gets heavy—a weight equal to thousands of historical layers—and for disembarking this heavy weight, I need to paint otherwise I would lose my mind," Resho finally broke the ice and revealed the Room of Inspiration.

He talked about the nature he communicates with and summons him in.

"Whenever I open the window, after a while, the Cat appears and sits on the edge. A black Cat with extremely bright eyes that gets me mesmerized with just a glimpse. It makes me close my eyes and, suddenly, images conjure up in my mind; images that can be embraced neither in colors nor in notes and not even in words. I just infer some images from them and put the colors on the canvas," Resho continued but he was in two minds about mentioning the Malik Tawus, the god of rebellion.

Resho saw that the girl's face is turning into a big eye full of smaller ones. Consequently, her life revolved around fixating on a single point while contemplating Resho, his Room of Inspiration, the window, the Cat, the girl, the voices, and the lifeless body beneath the oak tree.

Had she known that fate was perched nearby, waiting indifferently for her, she might have hurled herself down the exhibition's staircase, vanishing into the cyclical currents of history only to re-emerge two thousand years later. If she had delayed her departure by merely five minutes, she would have found herself wandering through the illuminated pathways of the future. Had she taken a different route to purchase a dress, she could have embarked on a voyage beyond the confines of her inner universe, stepping alongside her lover, hand in hand, along a seaside shore.

14

From which reservoir of truth did Resho's words emanate, creating a ripple that ensnared the girl's thoughts within intricate webs of both mental and spiritual enigmas? She struggled to fathom it, caught between disbelief and acceptance. Was it a dream or reality, an enchantment or a trance? This mental metamorphosis led her to an expanse of unanswered questions, rendering her adrift in an ocean of uncertainty.

Helpless, she found herself in a state of profound surrender to these unadulterated inspirations. Subsequently, her right hand instinctively cradled her chin, guiding her gaze into the depths of darkness.

She gathered all her belongings within a glass jar. For her, time bowed down, a serene lament upon the shell of a turtle.

Before encountering Resho at the exhibition, her smiles held a magnetic charm, drawing anyone near. Her zeal for producing paintings radiated from her very core. However, after that incident, her focus shifted entirely. All she desired was to clutch and tighten her hold on Resho's wellspring of inspiration. Resho's life appeared as a relieving abyss, while the girl now, present at his resting place, yearned for that same rebellious tranquillity.

She longed for the presence of a cat, a companion to guide her away from the realm of the mundane—a presence beyond earthly matters, untouched by the control of the relentless sun. Everything occurred under the sun, yet she sought the night, the moon, and the stars to illuminate her artistic path; these celestial elements held the potential to satiate her creative hunger.

After the painting exhibition, she sought out a place devoid of human presence, where their voices wouldn't intrude. She made her way to a garden of remembrance positioned to the north of their city, nestled at the base of a lofty mountain and amidst the oak woods. Her purpose was to experience the echoes of Resho's muses up close. A little above the cemetery, she settled beneath a tree that would later become Resho's solitary tree, gazing upon the majesty of the mountain. A robust wind swept through the air, its mournful cry intertwining with the mythical voices of two brothers. Her tongue felt muted as she mentally cast aside everything around her, immersing herself in the contemplation of what she had been told.

The crimson hue of the horizon bathed her eyes in an aura of mystery, while thoughts of Resho permeated her very essence. As the sun descended, the sky transformed from its fiery red to deep black. A few individuals arrived at the graveyard, seizing the opportunity to reconnect with their departed loved ones and rekindle their awareness of mortality. The wind persisted in its fervent blowing, lifting the dust and infusing the cemetery with an otherworldly quality. Within this dream-like atmosphere, trees, stones, and people underwent enigmatic metamorphosis. The eerie resonance of peculiar voices slithered through the forest, as if the deceased were engaged in a spectral choir.

The yellowish clouds loom behind the desiccated branches, exposing her pale, slender face. The red sun, nestled behind the hill of death, spills the sorrow of her eyes onto the mountain. Every element around her takes on the essence of Resho's existence. The Resho's Cat extends its grasp beyond the mountains, ascending to conquer the summit. It stares straight into the girl's eyes.

In haste, the girl ascended the mountaintop, gazing across to the other side—an urban settlement cradled within the depths of a vast valley. Thousands of people were gripped by panic, evacuating the city. They had been alerted to the impending bombardment and the genocide that had been decreed. Gunners had ensnared the city, barring any escape. Even those who attempted to flee were coerced back. The populace returned to their homes, seeking refuge within their basements. The sky transformed into darkness as the bombers unleashed their payload . . .

Filled with dread, the girl hastened back to the cemetery.

15

Omar Kawar: The Third Narrative

The girl yearns to visit the Room of Inspiration, where she can be fully immersed in the presence of the Cat and the window. However, her fascination with the realm of his writing is so consuming that she finds herself unable to resist the allure of reading.

Based on my previous dreams and the feeling that I had, I clearly knew all the people would be genocided, and I knew my impending dream would be about this event. I had a vision that they are to be sacrificed. Ambiguously, I have seen them setting off to the mountains in their immediate vicinity, with oaks in their hands, and they were vanished and lost in nature. So curious were I and I couldn't wait. I kept fidgeting with my chest hair. I wanted to envisage it so I wanted to know my close friends' ideas in order to make the jigsaw fall into place. Therefore, I sent them a letter and asked this question:

"Imagine that all the inhabitants in a city go to the mountains that surround their city to plant oak trees. These people, during past years, have been killed many times; have been subjected to brutal mass murder either in the hands of an outsider, an enemy, or in the hands of their own people in power: the serpents, the vultures, the traitors, the Jaash. This time, I believe even nature wants to doom them. Maybe by killing them all, nature wants to put an end to their suffering; a kind of mercy killing. You are given a mighty power to make nature kill them all. How would you do it?"

The thing that emotionally drew me closer to my girl and made me believe that we are mentally so close was her response to the letter.

The oaks are destroyed due to the intensely freezing cold. They are all in want of sun heat. The sun slowly emerges through the clouds and shines its light upon earth and the earthly. People are gradually feeling assured and their enthusiasm to plant oaks starts to grow.

The sun highlights its rays and they become reddish pink second by second. Then, they take off their clothes and lie on the ground nakedly. Comfortably numb, their backs are glued to earth with their bones and skins being mingled with soil. Little by little, their bodies are being liquefied; their hairs are burning. The oaks are also being melted and, together with people, they infiltrate into the earth. After a while, it rains and the saplings of the oaks are blooming out of the earth. So considerable are their growth that the soothing shadow of their leaves and branches darken the city in its entirety.

One of my good friends replied:

I don't kill them since they are all already dead. Every second of their lives is shadowed by death. Dead are they for being deprived of their homelands. Every corner of their city is occupied.

One of my friends who is a painter wrote back to me that:

The nearby mountains are high and covered by snow and oak trees. People, for being so tired of hiking, decide to have a short break under the oak trees. The oaks are beside them. Giant clusters of migrating birds are landing atop the mountains. The mountains are getting black and white. All the crows are singing and the snow shakes. Gargantuan masses of snow, brutally, are sliding down upon the sleeping people. They get suffocated under the snow but their missions are successfully done with the sprouting of the oaks. As saplings, they break through the snow and blossom out.

Another friend wrote:

I would turn the land under their feet and also the mountains into stone to suck their dream of planting oaks dry and make them die slowly.

Another one replied a bit late,

You can't take an oak to another land to plant it. Oaks only grow in their motherland. When they get ripe, people fetch the green ones and plant them in the same land.

I didn't know this fact about oaks so I got shocked. From that time on, this firm tree became more meaningful to me, and it made me love my own tree more.

One of my old friends:

If I ever happen to kill them, I would announce planting oak a big crime even the dreaming about which equalled their death. Hence, while planting and because of spreading nature, they are all chemically bombarded.

One of my friends who can't even imagine hurting an ant didn't reply to me though I have sent her letter many times. I forgot that she can never think of murdering someone let alone a nation. Only a person who has helplessly tasted malicious deeds can't even think of issues as such. I saw her and insisted so much that she said, "I prefer to be killed than to kill. I would take a sense from each one of them like hearing from one and sight from another. S/he who can't see helps the one who can't hear, so they form a unified body never to be killed by anyone, even nature."

Another friend:

Once I saw a snake biting a rat in my garden, then, noticing me, it went inside its hole. After an hour, I saw all its body covered by ants and it looked completely black. The body was being torn apart, and then every bit was taken to the anthill. If I were the one to kill those people, I would do it by ants; therefore, they could be spread in the heart of nature. Mother Earth could immortalize them.

An ocean of metaphors, images, and words were wandering in my mind until after some weeks Omar Kawar and the people of silent city came to my dream.

Omar Kawar has found a nook on a big branch of his tree. He is writing. Fidgeting with his knees, he tearfully stares at the city. He is reminded of the well he has seen before and draws his burning children on his notebook. He can hear their howl. He draws their faces and the blazes that stick their hair to their faces, all burning in fire.

Omar closes his notebook. He, along with his twin sons, is going toward the outdoor theatre which is located at the city center at the middle of a roundabout. There is a giant dried oak tree there. They are seemingly preparing the stage for an event. Omar is coming toward home and picking green oaks from the trees on his way. He ponders on the future when nature, his only tree, and his city are collapsing down in fire. As soon as getting home, he puts the fruits in water.

The day after, he gives each of his children an oak.

They have already budded.

"I want you my children to plant these oaks on the mounts around our city. We do this once a week. We have to plant all the mounts," he firmly commanded.

Their city is like a bowl— houses being at the bottom surrounded by high mountains. From above the mounts, the entire city is visible. The mounts with oak trees on their skin are the symbol of their city. People, on weekends, in long lines, hike the highest mountain.

People see Omar Kawar's family while planting oaks. Next week, all people with budded oaks are going to mounts. The city is fully evacuated. They are holding the oaks while being unaware that the buds are wildly growing. They twist around their hands and grow more. Like snakes ringing around a body, they twist around their necks and tighten themselves. All the people are getting suffocated and, after a while, their dead bodies start decomposing.

A heavy rain pours and they all melt inside the oak roots. The day after, oak trees rise to the sky in order not to let the sunshine on the city anymore.

I am in my grave and I feel my body being decomposed. I feel my being sucked by the roots and my growing with the oak tree trunks. When I was awakened, I felt a shadow, instead of sunshine, and I was so relieved that, as I can remember, I never experienced such a relaxation before.

Someone knocked the door all of a sudden. Anxiety seized me. I stood up but I got cold feet. I plucked my courage and opened the door. There was a woman standing at the door whose skin has turned black. Her skin was burnt. Her three kids have already died in her arms. She was coughing and foam sprouted through her mouth. He uttered some words but they were like the sound of a broken Tembur . . . "I won't let you live in peace . . . We won't loose our grips on you . . ." she said. Then she dropped a letter on the ground. A thick letter. Like a book. There were no signs on it. It had no cover. It wasn't clear who the sender was:

I am Omar Kawar. I am Omar Kawar. I am Omar Kawar. I am Omar Kawar. I am Omar Kawar. I am Omar Kawar. I am Omar Kawar. I am Omar Kawar. I am Omar Kawar. I am Omar Kawar. I am Omar Kawar. I am Omar Kawar. I am Omar Kawar. I am Omar Kawar. I am Omar Kawar. I am Omar Kawar. I am Omar Kawar. I am Omar Kawar. I am Omar Kawar. I am Omar

Kawar. I am Omar Kawar. I am Omar Kawar. I am Omar Kawar. I am Omar Kawar . . . We are all Omar Kawar. Omar Kawar did not die there in that spot. We were there. We are the true witnesses. Omar Kawar did not have his child in his arms. We saw it, Resho; but you didn't. His child was at home and Kawar was in another corner. They brought him and then . . . For an image, just for the sake of some damn pictures . . . They sacrificed a city . . . It was not nature which sacrificed us . . . It was some damn pictures. Grow up Resho, Why did you believe what you had seen? Don't ever make one person the symbol of Silent City. We are all Omar Kawar . . .

I counted them. Five thousand and twenty four "I am Omar Kawar" were written. They all signed the letter. I don't know. I never knew. I am confused. Their screams are deafening. I hear them all. I feel every pain they carried. It weathers away my spirit. Taus? Melek Taus? The god of this land, what shall I do? What my fault was? Is this path a wrong one? Then why did you put me in it? Was it you? Are my writings just a mirage? If they are all a mirage, then what? My dreams, shall I believe in them anymore? Are they true? Show yourself Taus, I am losing my mind.

16

She chose to continue painting alongside Resho, not solely for the purpose of mastering form and technique, but also to gain access to Resho's wellspring of inspiration—the Room of Inspiration, the window, and the Cat. While she had acquired the former, the latter remained elusive. Her entire existence had transformed into an aspiration to encounter it firsthand. Resho, however, always maintained a barrier between her and his room, never extending an invitation.

The girl yearned for the very essence of inspiration to sweep into her life. When Resho accepted her proposition to collaborate, their aim was to elevate their artistic prowess, bringing it closer to the sublime nature they sought to capture. This decision was not devoid of emotion. The sentiment that had taken root within their hearts intertwined their destinies with a potent force.

Once the seeds of love had taken root within him, Resho's life blossomed anew. He became attuned to the intricate dance of ants, the lantern's flickering light guiding his movements and causing his hair to surrender more readily to the caress of the wind. Inside his room, the oak tree's roots extended further, while the melodies produced by his Tanbur grew more mellifluous. The taste of tea became more pronounced, and the cigarette smoke assumed a deeper shade of blue. The ink in his pen seemed endless as he filled page after page with stories of Omar Kawar and the Silent City. His memory sharpened, capturing the minutest details of his dreams.

Resho walked upon the earth with bare feet, dedicating himself to the planting of more oak trees. He embraced the scent of wet bricks more fervently than before, using it to craft sentences that resonated with a deeper understanding of his homeland's history.

Resho wove the girl's words into a tapestry of colors, and over time, he noticed that his world had transformed into a spectrum of vibrant hues. Both he and the girl understood that their connection was more than mere love; it was an inspirational bond, a force that propelled them to offer each other greater incentives, guiding them towards the discovery of their individual paths and inspiring the creation of artworks that could elevate their emotions to new heights.

Resho held the belief that love demanded a higher quality—a quality of connection that extended beyond the conventional. Fearless, he approached the sun, unafraid of the allure of the forbidden fruit. Should he seize the pomegranate from the Tree of Life, he would bite into it with ravenous hunger, devouring even its skin. In this journey, the girl had also ventured into this paradise of uncharted exploration and boundless creativity. (In the next novel, you will see the girl getting pregnant by simultaneously painting under a tree and swallowing a pomegranate.)

He trusted his girl and step by step, they desired to propel their works toward nature. He used to remind his girl that the ups and downs of their mother land, the rebellious mountains of their Nishtiman should determine the rhythm of their artistic works. "None of us, none of our people has ever respected our land, no one has ever known the value of our rocky mountains," Resho said with an anger suppressed in his throat. "We don't deserve this Nishtiman. We simply let them, the others, to tear our mountains with their bulldozers. We, all of us, let them build their military bases on the peaks. We even provided them with the stones of our rocks. We let them build a big eye up there to scrutinize us."

The girl said nothing but she was all ears. "We should keep writing, painting, and making music so much, so much to compensate for our folly," Resho continued.

Resho firmly believed in the unification of Kurdewari's spirit and that of the Kurdish people. However, he couldn't help but wonder why the people were no longer as rebellious as they had been before, considering the wild and untamed nature of the mountains that surround them.

He used to say that all the spirits of creatures in universe are embodied, as a compact disk, inside human. "Our paintings should be nature incarnate," Resho said. "By doing so, we could pay our debts back to sublime nature. But as you see our nature is now wounded and looted."

His ideas redefined her beliefs about art. She just realized that ideas and contents must be able to quiver the world. Form, for Resho, was a tool to serve content and the content of his paintings were always Kurdish. "As far as our nature is sacked and torn into pieces, as far as it is divided among newly-established nation-states, the form of our works should also be, I mean, they have to be fragmented. Just like our nature, our mother, our country, which is shattered."

He possessed profound concepts that were meant to be translated onto canvas by the girl. He delved into her mind, discerning her thoughts, and articulated something that resonated with her internal musings. "A girl," Resho suggested. "As if dead, has fallen on a stone by a beach. Her head has been bleeding; maybe this is the blood of her thought that is reddening the nature. Resho told her it should be painted in a manner that expresses these feelings. Her hair has been poured in the shallow water and blackened a circular range of the sea. Red, blue, and black mixed. Her thoughts have transfigured the color of sea into red and its reflection devours the blueness of the sky. These ideas have already penetrated inside the sun; for that reason, it tends to orange. This painting must convey a sense to watcher that all nature is whirling with the suppressed beliefs of the figure."

She never mixed these colors on canvas. Instead, she gave Resho an idea for a painting.

The girl's suggestion ignited an idea within Resho, one that left him momentarily frozen in a state of profound awe. He found himself unable to move for a while.

The notion depicted a man whose physical form had diminished to a degree that he could perch on a turtle's shell, cradling a bird within his palm. The turtle advanced at such a leisurely pace that it seemed as though it rode atop the very shell of time itself, causing the passing days to remain in a motionless state.

Resho's mind harkened back to his childhood, recalling a wounded turtle that had toppled onto its shell. The creature, its gaze carrying an awareness preceding death, met his eyes. In that moment, he sensed that the girl possessed a metaphorical window through which she could peer into Resho's world. With each passing day, the similarities between their experiences grew, and Resho's apprehension of these parallels intensified.

17

The girl is still there on the grave with the notebook in her left hand. Resho has written some pages about her, and she is perusing them. She presses her fragile fingers against the pages of the notebook. Her long black hair is a part of the darkness of night. No sun is there above her head to agonize her. Waves of night that blow her hair, mingled with the sublime voice of the Brothers of Time, fall upon the branches of oak trees. Their roots twist around Resho's body, and she feels a shivering beneath her feet. The Brothers are observing her, but she feels their presence. She doesn't raise her head to watch them lest they vanish. For her peace of mind, she is in need of their soothing presence.

During those days, Being with Resho gave the girl zeal to live. She felt her heart sprouting new buds. Being with anyone except Resho was intolerable for her. She was been invited to the Centre of Universe, and, as gratitude, she wanted to grant him a painting, one of her best ones—a painting which was the first manifesto of her universe inside, and her relieving loneliness was initiated by this painting.

When I saw this painting, I faced a truth of how alike we really do think and how many things we both have in common. I didn't want to invite her to come over to my room—the Centre of Universe. I don't know if it was right or wrong, but still I wish I would never get acquainted with her. I wish the burning trace of experience would never be constituted in my girl's mind. She deserves to breathe and smell aromatic flowers.

Day by day, she becomes more secluded, and I blame myself. I don't mean that the inner feeling of loneliness is destructive, but it can be heavier as time passes. It makes the time-age unison scrambled the unscrambling of which results in demise; then, you will find nobody to bury you and to attend your funeral. It takes youth from you. It shows you future, and this signifies confronting a truth which ends up being disallowed by society

Why has she painted herself as three lonely models in the prisonhouse of her thought? A jail satiated in surrealistic images; a jail in which life elements have been portrayed in a dream-like manner. The three girls in the painting look at you in way as if they want to drag you inside their isolation. The three girls are the three drops of blood of their creator; three girls, though being together, are melted in their being marooned.

My girl is a person in whose loneliness she talks with her divided self. She considers herself as three people being obliged to keep themselves quarantined by their outside world. They never wish to escape from their dream land. This picture is actually a mimesis of her inner mind. She is the one who has closed the framework of her poetic imagination to everyone. She fears the cold and the ice outside.

An oak tree's shadow is engraved on the prison wall; a shadow under which floating fishes are born inside an orange carpet. One of the tree girls sadly hugs her knees, and her naked essence is dissolved into the nude fishes of the world of fantasies.

The other one in complete black mourns for her detachment from the interactions of surrounding world. That other one with navy blue dress is gazing at the wine glass poured on the ground seeming that she regrets her poured age. She is totally estranged from her two other selves.

The girl closes the notebook, exhaling a cold sigh. She intertwines her fingers and takes a seat, lighting a cigarette. Her gaze fixates on the wisps of blue smoke spiralling from the cigarette, her thoughts drifting to the day she crossed the threshold into the Center of the Universe. That encounter with Resho marked the inception of her journey into the realm of pure art—an art born of profound solitude, not intended for mere visual appeal and people's attention, but to fill the inner void, permeated by the aroma of wet bricks.

As her cigarette nears its end, a yearning wells within her to delve further into Resho's words, eager to witness her memories come alive upon his grave through his words.

This familiarity was Janus-faced. As I was getting out of my seclusion, she was tending, from outside word, to step inside her inner universe.

I never let her walk inside the Room of Inspiration because I don't want her to get more secluded. Description of the room and the Cat has mesmerized her enough, so I let our looks convene at the Centre of Universe.

When her foot touched the floor, my last fears were broken with the halo of the cigarette smoke—fears which have been clawing deep inside of me since childhood, fears which closed this room's door to the world to let myself plant the seeds of wild dreams. A feeling that was formed out of deep fears and anxieties, with her entering the room, transferred to tranquillity and its aroma encompassed all the room. The painting she brought with her has melted my tough and stone-like psyche. When she walked on the floor, my inner ocean shivered and its shakes has untied my knitted paradoxes.

Her canvas made the centrality of my room impeccably impenetrable. The burning tune of Tanbur was echoing in the room, the lights died, our faces mingled with faint light of the candles, and our internal feelings infected the atmosphere of the room. There were no longer a place for logic and rationality, feeling was dominant.

If we place a jar at the middle of desert, all the sands will tend to dance to get the form of the jar. A true work of art can even harmonize the wildly indifferent nature with itself. Her painting, likewise, metamorphosed the structure and form of my room.

I felt the world spinning in our arms; I was unaware if rivers convened when I ringed my hands around her; I didn't know whether it rained there for children dying of thirst at the end of world when I kissed her forehead. I didn't know, but I could feel it; I could feel it with my bone and flesh that, with our lovemaking, children of the Silent City were smiling. She came to revolutionize me and the world. My words and I are haunted since she is herself the inspirational muse; she is coming from the land of my Tawus. I never even whisper her name to my friends. I never brought her name here in these words. She is gonna be called and read. She shouldn't have any name since so delicate is she that language would viciously splinter her.

Loneliness is the greatest grace of my life and, to me, she is herself loneliness embodied in human flesh. She hasn't come to fill it; she has come to deepen it.

She is sent from him, I feel it with all my cells. She has come to blacken my papers.

The girl smiles and presses a kiss onto the notebook's pages, sealing her connection with its contents.

18

Just like the wind shifts borders, Resho's life had these waves that stirred like the sands of a desert. But he was dead set on defining his life as an artist in a certain way. He was a real rebel, and his whole vibe had a direct impact on me too. A single thunderclap and lightnin' strike could upend his entire existence. Dude used to roll with the river's flow, ride on notes in the air, and have the wind as his life's role model. He ain't never really had specific wishes, and he'd cook up a plan for his future only every now and again. As a result, any old breeze could just whisk his mind off to a Nowheresville.

Every now and then, he'd make his way to the terminal, just watchin' them buses come and go. Folks were all travelin' for a purpose, a reason. But there was Resho, posted up, starin', lost in thought. He was wishin' he could break free from boundaries, hop on a bus to anywhere, just to find a moment of bein' unknown, to live in pure obscurity. His top-tier adventure was walkin' through unfamiliar alleys, under them wanderin' stars. See, Resho's homeland, his Nishtiman, it was occupied, colonized. That's why he wrote. That's why he was tangled up in his thoughts.

One of his texts still hangs up on my room's wall (For real? My room's wall? Am I going mad?).

Lines of buses ready to depart
Drowned in bright lights
In the heart of the night
Waiting for passengers
From the land of estrangement
One gets inside eternity

One inside destiny

One inside bad luck

One desires immortality

One wants mortality

In this chaos

I am left

Ticketless

Packing my bag

And walking to distant lands

Of nostalgia,

Melancholy,

And amnesia.

He had a real thing for wildlife, like he'd just get lost in the world of animals. Whenever he spotted one, he'd be over the moon (I mean, really, over the moon). He had a special spot for the colorful critters, like snakes, that was his jam.

One time, I summoned Resho up. He was deep in contemplation, and I could feel what was on his mind. Right before he could even start talkin', I beat him to it, spillin' out the exact words that were on his mind: "Man, I wish I could eavesdrop on animals chattin' 'bout us humans. They ain't too fond of us, no doubt. They'd be sayin', 'Why's some Kurdish folk lettin' these absurd colonizers run the show?' Oh, picture it, a snake just chillin', laughin' at me, or you. How'd a whole people let outsiders roll in and do 'em harm?" That was the very first time in my whole life I seen Resho bust out laughin'. I really wanted him to laugh so I added a bit of sarcasm to the snake's speech: "I be chillin' in my own spot, and when hunger hits, I step out and scavenge in my hood. Anyone who messes with me, they become my enemy, and I pounce on 'em, bite 'em, sting 'em. In the worst-case scenario, I might meet my end, but I ain't goin' down without a fight, and death be better than bein' locked up. I can't figure out why them Kurds act this way. They be dead in their own land, end up as refugees, and even in their own hood, they feel like outsiders. I don't get why they done made me their symbol at all. Their stories be filled with my presence: the King of the Snakes, The Black Snake, and other crazy tales. I'm tellin' ya, I'm feelin' real ashamed of myself."

Another time, he had this dream of bein' a shepherd in a land filled only with sheep; just vibin' with their company. He'd be there, soaking in their innocence, a spot with no hint of fake. Nobody'd play him, no one'd be tryna pull one over on him. "Sheep never lie," Resho said. "They don't know what painting is, there is no art to diddle people's skirts, and to go up a notch in social status, there are no cultural masks in this utopia of sheep. Culture, language, and ideology can't categorize them. What a borderless place it can be, a place where the sheep, due to their colorlessness, could be a source of colorful inspirations. Their looks are so full of simplicity, innocence, and empathy that can help create hundreds of complex works of art." His tone was drippin' with sarcasm. He was like, if he ever ended up in a spot like that, he could peep the world through the eyes of a sheep, and it'd be all kinds of perfect.

He always had this sayin', wishin' he could settle down in a far-off village, way off the beaten path, with some sheep, maybe even be a sheep himself, just chillin' and thinkin' 'bout munchin' on grass. Anywhere where plants and tree leaves grew could be his own kind of paradise. No fear of pain or heartache, and he wouldn't even know what it's like to worry. Shoot, he didn't even know when or why he might end up bein' slaughtered. Them sheep, they ain't got a clue 'bout what it means to have a nation without a state. Genocide and assimilation? Nah, that ain't in their wheelhouse. And that feelin' of bein' in your own city, yet feelin' like a total stranger? Nope, they ain't got a lick of that.

Oh my damn goodness gracious, my very own personal god, only I know the pain that Resho was bearin'.

Resho believed folks ain't all that different to be causing all this separation. Each person, compared to the vastness of their mind, they got a confined space of meanin'. A farmer, he truly gets the colors of the land, while a gravedigger, his grasp of life don't go beyond a grave. But he sure understands the spirit of death, no doubt.

Plato and his granny, in Resho's eyes, they're practically cut from the same cloth. They got this giant resemblance goin' on. Plato's doin' his thing back in 428 BC, while his grandma's holdin' it down in the 20th century. And then you got Shakespeare, cookin' up his plays back in the 16th century. Thing is, neither Plato nor his grandma's got a chance to read his stuff, so they're on an even keel.

He held them humanistic views, but there was a mirage in play 'cause society didn't exactly embrace him with open arms. He was convinced that the soil, the earth, the whole shebang he called mother earth, well, that belonged to the people; that the land of the Kurds shouldn't be sliced and claimed by others. The Kurdish folks should be free on their own land. He wasn't really buyin' into nation-states and borders, but the whole dang world, every country, was sportin' one, so why not the Kurds with their 60 million-plus souls? Yet, folks kinda brushed these truths aside and carried on like slaves. Society, it never gave him that nod of acceptance. Over time, it hit him like a brick, and he wandered into isolation. Them societal expectations, they peeled his masks off one by one. The more he stepped away from the crowd, the closer he got to his art. Eventually, he sorta melted right into his own essence, open to moments of inspiration that cut real deep.

His girl, she owned up to that truth too, and them smiles of hers stopped unfoldin', them smiles that used to shine like a beautiful flower. They was facin' them repercussions of bein' rebellious Kurdish artists; Resho layin' low below, his girl standin' strong on the ground.

Folks just couldn't quite grasp Resho 'cause of his words and actions. He'd chat up a storm, no real game plan, not carin' 'bout the words he chose. He'd put his feelings out there, no filter, nothin'. To me, that's what made Resho the real deal (or human? Shoot, I ain't got a solid answer. I just wish we had more Reshos in our homeland, folks who could really smell the damp bricks). Dude never spun a web of lies. He just couldn't rein in his thoughts. And that's why his words sometimes got tangled up, 'cause he'd unknowingly think in this twisty way, mixin' up tenses, even in his writings. I never did no editin' on 'em.

(Truth be told, he wasn't the one talkin' all vague. Nah, it was them folks who weren't keepin' it clear enough to get what he was sayin'. Resho, he had a clear grip on the fact that Kurdewari was under a heavy colonial thumb, and he knew what had gone down with the people. He was hip to why folks had slipped into forgetfulness. He'd chat 'em up all the time, tryna shed light on the truths 'bout their land and culture. But they'd brush his words aside, spoutin' stuff like, "It's a global thing, happens everywhere." After a while, he just went silent. He became the loneliest cat, takin' shelter in the world of his words and his Tembur.)

Just like someone strugglin' with aphasia, gettin' the theme of words all jumbled up, he'd switch 'em around, messin' with that straight line of meanin'. Resho, man, he was a poet, a thinker. He'd mix up them word sequences to shake up the history folks had laid down.

His life was like a rollercoaster, ridin' them wild ups and downs, just like our homeland's geography. It's all about them high mountains, and anyone who goes all-in, just like Resho, ends up wild at heart. Dude got himself lost in them peaks and the wild outdoors, a total surrender. He bet it all on bein' himself, on bein' one with the mountains, on bein' musical notes. But it ended up bein' sorta lethal. At least that's how I see it, kinda like a self-wanted death. Resho dug it, he hungered for it, gave his all for it, and he laid his life down for it. I ain't wantin' to say I took his life. He went towards it willingly. The path he chose, well, it led to death and he was fully aware of it.

He'd head over to Jamkhana once a week, regular as rain. There, he'd be strummin' on that Tembur with 'bout twenty other folks or so. Couple old heads might be workin' that beat with a Daf, I'd be right there rollin' with him too. Whole bunch of old cats would be dancin' up a storm, doin' that Sama and gettin' into the Dhikr. The Daf's rhythm, it'd spirit him away to the mountains; same kinda rise and fall, like those peaks. He'd be gettin' down, his long wavy hair swayin', like a gust of wind up on that mountain peak.

19

Omar Kawar: The Fourth Narrative

I have no idea regarding why I have stepped there. Fiscal and spiritual matters compelled me to live there. The condition in which I have been was, on one side, a deep dark vortex, and, on the other side, high and eye-scratching rocks. I must have found a way out or I would literally face my demise. More terribly, the place I moved next has made me pick my chest hair more and I kept fidgeting with my fingers.

I wish I could nest in dorm. There either I couldn't breathe. No on tolerated me and neither could I stand them. I needed to be alone to grow my ideas, and let my thoughts get brown. Had I been in my room in my city, I would have seen my Cat every night and that could suffice. This very room here has no window. The only sound I can hear is the voice of children playing in the alley.

I stand in front of the blank canvas. With the hope of not seeing and hearing the kids on the way back home, I get dressed and go out of the spiritless home. I wish they could sleep soon. These children are planting my spirit with seeds of destruction.

The alleys here are so narrow that bicycles can't move comfortably. Oh my inspirational angel, children rain from every corner and on every wall and tree. They sit on the branches and they scream aloud. I wish trees here were oak. Not even a pomegranate tree exists here in this quagmire . . . If there was, I would tie myself to the tree by a rope . . .

Why do they all resemble each other? When I look at them, I remember the children of Silent City with the same heavy looks. My mind gets heavy and I am unable to close my eyes. I think the children of Silent City are conjuring up. Oh the god of languages, what shall I do with all these children on the walls and trees? They all, with their burnt faces, keep staring at me. Stumbling inside these tiny and narrow alleys, I can't get rid of their cat-like eyes.

I run home. Helplessly, I run toward home through the labyrinthine and claustrophobic alleys. They are like mazes resembling dreadful tunnels on the top of which cat-like kids are sitting.

I approached home. I saw a wise old man sitting on a stone in the alley. I felt he would know the reason for the existence of those overabundant children. I could guess he was Taus, and I went straight home. He was staring at me. I could feel the weight of his look on my knees.

As soon as arriving home, I packed up. I had nothing but the painting of the girl and my Tamira— the mere possessions of mine. I stepped out of home and headed straight to terminal. I couldn't go back to university since the head of department has approved my resignation letter. My going back home became the turning point of my life. The declivity of my life sharpened its angle, ninety nine times sharper. I felt something was summoning me, something made of words and nature.

I was about to arrive in my city. I got out and walked toward my Room of Inspirations. The city's atmosphere, architecture, and even nature have remarkably changed phantasmagorically. Everything was in the house of my dreams. A dark light shone on the city which made me close my eyes. In a blink, I found myself where the Brothers of Time were born.

They are born again. As soon as coming out of their mother's stomach, the scream of thousands of people reverberates in the city and the room as well. Thousands of wandering souls are flying in the sky and, after coming inside the room, they enter the mind of the twin brothers.

I saw the clock hands turning so speedy, I felt like falling in the vortex of time. I saw diverse images: picture of oak trees that have blossomed, children standing in line and being thrown inside deep and big holes, a girl standing on a grave reading a notebook, the Brothers of Time singing elegy on a grave under a dried oak tree, me scratching the wall plasters and wetting the bare bricks, Tamuras breaking under debris and their breaking and cracking voices sent shiver down the spine of earth, the fire rain that lighted the city in the dark, a hairy old man sitting on Omar Kawar's mind, and I, once again, saw myself on Mohammad Shwan's grave.

Omar Kawar and his seven daughters who have aged are standing on Mohammad Shwan's tomb. The Brothers of Time are going to organize the theatre stage. They have a show on the weekend. Omar Kawar unbuttoned his shirt. He had been picking his chest hair so frantically that become hairless like a wall with no plaster.

In his deep pocket, he takes a notebook out. He tells his children about a text he has written yet not complete. Tells them that it was for a while that he saw strange dreams which put a heavy burden on his mind. He said that the dreams followed each other up like series; he wrote the dreams and wanted to perform a show on stage. He asked his family to enact it together.

He said he saw a man in his dreams, a terrific man with specks of color on his hands. He said the man was dead but gave his sight to a familiar girl who was doomed to stand on his grave reading the story of his life.

He told his family the summary of the story:

"This play is about a painter whose name's Resho. A mysterious old man obliges him to give the voice of a nation which has been genocided to the world, so he makes him write. After the old man's appearance in his life, Resho sees heavy dreams that should be written. He is so deeply involved in his mission that he walks out on everybody even the girl and his best friend named Sirwan who were his only confidants. He has written parts of his mission, and he decides to live beside his oak tree at the heart of an oak jungle so that he can finish it. Another significant part of his life is about the girl.

She, by accident, goes to his painting exhibition and becomes so enchanted by his works. She asks him about where he gets his inspiration. Responding to this question is Resho's greatest secret. He confides in her and mentions his Room of Inspiration whose window opens to a sublime nature of high mountains and an oak jungle; tells her about a Cat that comes inside the window and inspires him. After this discussion, the girl gets mesmerized and her eyes become magical.

The girl wants to bring Resho back to social life and intends to paint a masterpiece for him. Due to being exposed to intense and heavy inspirations, Resho, by doing his mission, and Sirwan, by turning Resho's mission and his life into a story, have lost their minds. After some months, Sirwan, who witnessed Resho's death, goes to see the girl to tell her about him. Tells her about a dream he saw and the girl, ignorant of the heavy rain, restlessly leaves her house with the painting in her hands. She gets to Resho's dead body. Digs the ground and buries Resho. She puts the blank canvas on his tomb as gravestone.

I have written these parts of Resho's life, and I'm waiting for next dreams."

This narrative wasn't a dream. I meant it. I went toward my room but stepped inside the Silent City instead and ended up here beside my tree which is being dried day by day. I hugged it.

I am petrified Tawuse Melek, so much afraid. Oh my god of inspiration, what is happening to me? I can't believe that Omar Kawar has seen my death. It is difficult for me to leave my mission unfinished.

You yourself created me and you were unknowingly haunted by me. Now you want to shake me off? What did you want from me? Did you want me to get to know yourself? Did you want me to revive the dead of our land? Did you want me to take back every inch of our colonized land? Ok. I did the former but why are you taking my life in the middle of my mission?

After this event, Resho found himself in a state of catatonic numbness. He yearned to bring his narratives to fruition, and with each passing second of his life, he longed to glimpse Tawus, the deity of death and rebirth, and the visions that awaited him in the next dream.

20

The girl decides, after reading this chapter of Resho's writing, to directly go to the second to last narrative of Omar Kawar in his notebook since she can't tolerate the burning burden of waiting. She wants to visit the Room of Inspiration and the Cat as soon as possible and to continue reading the Resho's words (the other two novels of this trilogy) there.

I didn't want to die. I wanted to live, to live like a shoemaker: to be happy with a loaf of bread, to get excited with a little scrambling of the mundane. The descending of heavy and petrifying inspirations took me to the undying demise of the fractals of my fragile life. From that time on, nothing makes me happy, nothing does wonder me either, my physic moves not, since I roam the world in my mind. Like a person who experiences everything and wants to commit suicide just to know death, my adventurous spirit has fully wandered universe. For a person who has been to the land of death, living on this very earth no longer excites him.

For a soul like Resho, who's caught wind of the wet bricks and grasped what's gone down in his homeland, it's a whole other level of tough to coexist with folks who ain't walked that path. They just don't get it, their minds stuck in the grip of colonization, their blood movin' slow and hard like stone.

I done gone to see Resho many a time, knockin' on his door like a broken record, but he ain't open up. I'd start thinkin', maybe he'd put an end to it all. I needed him for this story's endin'. One time, I was so dang on edge, I had to scale that door like a mountain climber. I burst into his room. There he was, sittin', just lost in his own thoughts. Not a word from his lips, like some kinda ascetic on a fast of silence. Them walls, they was decked out with paintings and snapshots of Omar Kawar and the Children of Silent City. Resho's pain, it came from knowin' the truth 'bout their lives, the lives of two hundred thousand and twenty-four souls buried alive, and them others gone from them

95

chemical gases. I swear, it was like they was hauntin' him. He turned into this kind of melancholic madman, and he was even happy 'bout it. He wasn't alone no more, could chat up the whole lot. He said he wanted to set up shop right in the heart of the jungle, by his lonesome oak tree.

I have lost the power of my speech. Sometimes, not a word is uttered from my mind. My girl is always asking me if she has done something wrong, and I always say that you have no fault. I wish she could understand that by each word flowing on my tongue a piece of my being is detached. If I abandon all and get myself surrendered to high mountains and the oak tree, I will no longer be obliged to talk. I wish she could understand that by uttering a single word a day is reduced from my life. I wish she knew that I don't want language with all its failings to mediate between us. It can't convey my feelings, my thoughts to her. I want to go on a lifelong fast. This prison house can't unleash my deep concerns, so how can I trust this very greatest invention of human beings? Tawus, the god of the earth and the earthly, has made me undergo a linguistic mission but words can't express genocide and the burning of children. I am now like a deaf-and-dumb person who knows a truth and wants to notify his people that the others are coming to kill us all.

I am getting accustomed to writing. In people's absence I can use this linguistic feature more. Their presence limits me. While being alone, I can write about everything, but when I feel a person beside me, I am no longer me and I censor my mind. To talk means to feel the presence of audience and to form a dialogue full of limits.

I want to put aside my words for the burnt children, for writing the last pages of a city's narrative which will rise from its ashes, the narrative of Omar Kawar and all the two hundred thousand and twenty four people who would celebrate, with blossoming of the trees, the revival of nature. In stark contrast, obligatorily, they linger here in my recluse and chaotic mind. They achieved freedom, though in my words. I hope Sirwan can get their voice to the world.

I can envisage future since the mundane hole has dissolved me. Being alone, listening to those same songs, looking at these same objects, sitting on the same rug in the same room of the same house, and gazing at the same figures of the same paintings on the same rough walls has made my mind so incredibly melancholic that washing it away necessitates death. Death only can break this linear life.

My paintings on the wall, these spirits incarcerated in colors, are but companions of my loneliness. They are survivors of a history in which its hangmen, by reading a verse from their holy book, have shed blood; however, they don't know they are not dead, they never die. Once again, they will smell the earth, the wet earth.

These people have witnesses the unknowable tensions of history, but, from the time I painted them and wrote about them, I can see smiles on their burnt faces. The Brothers of Time have penetrated in my dreams, and they sing a song whose resonance echoes throughout the woods.

Always, when I open my eyes, the clock, by showing 11:11, intensifies my sublime fear, and then I listen to the creaking sound of the wooden window till it gets quite wide open. The Cat with his bright and big eyes comes over inside the window to magnify my isolation with his transcendent inspirations. This is when I take shelter in my memories with my girl.

I take shelter in my memories which are fading to black, in the restless and chirping symphony of our kisses while the whole earth was spinning with our lovemaking. But this division between us. I don't know what it is. From the very beginning, I told her that love is not the only thing I crave for. I wanted difference; I wanted her to paint beside me for hours; I wanted to plant more depth of feeling. She was the only one who could break the shallowness of my mind. Her red lips could be the greatest source of inspiration. Her curved body could give gestural shapes to my works. I could motivate her to paint more, to contribute to our history. But this division between us. The more she got nearer to me, the less she could mix colors, and this was my biggest fear from the inception of our relation.

She was infected by a mental stasis, as if her inspirations were sucked dry. I gave her ideas, but she couldn't color the canvas. I feel regret for her poetically fragile feelings that could make a movement in painting. But she is spoiling her abilities. I wish I never saw her. I feel guilty. This is my fault. I have taken her hands so many times to tell her that these hands are not granted to everybody. Tears speechlessly inundated her eyes. Her eyes. Her smiles. Her body. Her ideas. But this division between us. The more she keeps silence, the more I feel I belong to the wild nature. The nature beyond the window, the oak trees, and the high mounts are summoning me. I obviously feel it.

After burning all my paintings, my isolation got complete then my speech got locked. I could no longer live in society, among people.

The leaves,

The branches of your dreams,

Get relieved

When the heat of the morning tank

Can't be felt anymore

And you become a part of eternity

To feel your cells

Melting inside the worms

and the snakes

Ain't nothin' but death that could put a halt to Resho's mind wanderin'. He turned into somethin' like an old man dealin' with that heavy solitude, but he still had a glimmer of light. The only light in Resho's world was when he could write 'bout them gone. He found real joy when he wrapped up his mission. His one wish was that I could carry on with his task and spread it far and wide across the world.

21

Omar Kawar: The Fifth Narrative

Taking deep breaths with her eyes closed, the girl reflects on all of Resho's writings. She envisions his charred paintings and finds it difficult to believe. Words and colors dance beneath her closed eyelids. When she opens her eyes, she gazes at the grave. Having read portions of his notebook, she feels a lightheartedness akin to a feather floating in the wind. With this newfound lightness, she continues her journey.

I sat on the largest branch of Omar Kawar's oak tree watching the slumber city. It was five o'clock. A harsh sound, more frightening than the one in Armageddon when good and evil collide, awoke the Silent City. The whistling bombs, falling on the trot, broke windows, and the glasses were shattered to bits as waterfall. The city was gilded by the moonlight. I never even imagined being afraid of beauty.

People, stranded and aware of their fate, rushed out and swept up the broken pieces of glass. They met each other for the last time.

They went back to bed again.

I looked at my watch, it was winter. I was at Omar Kawar's house. All of them were asleep. The Brothers of Time were sleeping with their eyes wide open. Omar was frantically walking across the hall. He was afraid lest his nightmare would come true. He put on clothes and kissed his nine children goodbye and, with tearful eyes and agitated heart, headed straight to the mountain and his tree. Sittings on his tree, he beheld the city. I was some steps away from him. He reclined and went into a deep sleep. He slept like a log in a way that he didn't hear the bombing booms. A dying dog was barking and he woke up. Went down the tree while feeling terribly light-headed. Appalled and nauseous, he watched his ruined city whose sky was blackened by the thick clouds of smoke.

The stench of apple has encompassed everywhere and encroached on everybody's mind. He looked around and saw all the oak trees had fruited apples, black and rotten apples. His eyes were burning, his sight was fading to black, and his pupils were shrinking. Irregularly and with difficulty, he breathed, and he couldn't handle his muscles. He coughed up a pink liquid and the white, brown, and green nature turned pink and bloody red. He collapsed but the image of his dying children didn't let him die. Raised his catatonic body, and stumblingly kept going. I took his hand but couldn't help him.

Beside a spring, he saw a little girl. She was naked and her skin, like a wall under which a fire was blazing, had deep cracks. Her skin was so fragile that it burnt down as glass. The cracks opened and Omar Kawar saw her flesh and white bones. Her whole body disjointed and spread over the ground.

Omar Kawar knew he would die in mere minutes. He was walking four legs down the mountain. Nature was decomposing the bodies, and he couldn't believe nature was that cruel. He sensed the cold death creeping in his legs. Wind blew and death was sowing its seeds on the Silent City.

He took a road heading to the city and, thereafter, he witnessed a three-year-old boy lying like a burnt doll between his parents. His father has put his left arm under his head, so his son would die more peacefully. Around the corpses, there was flowing a pink liquid.

He saw a father dying in his son's arms. He saw a mother whose daughter had become the continuation of her breasts. He saw a bride resting in wedding gowns, and her groom who was alive and laughing. Giggled and coughed blood.

Omar wasn't aware, but I could see that on one of the rooftops, seven old men and women had burnt themselves while dancing and praying Dhikr. Their long hair was also swaying with the ups and downs of their heads. Tiny flames from the fire were scattering onto the neighboring alleys and onto us as well. Their bodies were all burnt except for their bones. They had been dancing without any music. Suddenly, all of them fell off the edge and spread out on the ground.

Then, he saw a boy in an alley sitting under an oak tree. His family has passed away before his eyes. While writing something, the boy was taking his last breaths. Omar went nearer.

"I couldn't accomplish my mission," the boy whispered into his ears, "The god *of languages won't forgive me."*

He died and Omar read his lines:

Rain clusters of bullets

Pouring on

The innocence wheat land

Of this nation's saturation in loneliness.

'We grow wheat again,'

My father said.

The petrifying sound of bullet's horror

Could not

Settle people in the seclusion of their minds.

I could feel

My mother lies in peace

Nature gets her back and

The roots of oak trees

Have hugged her dead body.

I saw

My brother

Atop the mountain

With his instrument

With his Tamura

With the burning sound of his music

With a lantern in his hands

Is in search of freedom

Beyond the eye-scratching mountains.

My sister

Pouring her hands' blood on glued-to-earth faces

Of children

So Mother Earth

Would protect them.

I am sowing the last drops of my imagination

To return from beyond death

Mosquitos

Flies

Snakes

Worms

Vultures

Are pouring my blood drops

All over the world

To suck my beliefs dry

Beliefs that hid revolution inside themselves

Beliefs that would turn the collective grudges

Into the crystal seeds of freedom

Beliefs that could propagate immortality

The world is full of me

I can feel it

By shedding my soul

They have planted the seeds of their destruction.

He put the paper in his pocket and kept going. He was reminded of his own old man.

He arrived at the city theatre located in the heart of the city. The stage, meticulously arranged by the Brothers of Time, lay in ruins—what was once a room adorned with tables and chairs showcasing my paintings on the wall, a withered oak tree bearing a blank canvas beneath it, Dafs and Tamburs suspended from its branches, and a window housing a doll cat. All of these elements were engulfed in flames.

More than thirty people with masks stood on the platform of the theatre. They injected the vials and then commenced the prayer ceremony—funeral prayers. They were aware of the impending bombardment and had prepared themselves for this day. As they went into prostration, the masks prevented their foreheads from touching the ground; they dared not remove them.

Some others also arrived, once again wearing masks. They administered the vials and then brought out several corpses, arranging them according to their intentions. The platform became filled with the lifeless bodies of children, each one cradled in the arms of another seemingly deceased father or mother.

Photographers had infiltrated the city, positioning themselves as the primary witnesses to this grim scene. Like vultures, they clung to the ground, patiently awaiting the perfect opportunity.

Omar Kawar keeps moving and sees many other different scenes in his difficult journey. He no longer feels anything; cold is he like a stone on a mountain under snow. He just observes and nothing more. Can't cry. Can't be sad. Can't feel anything. Can't think about anything. He even can't think about the things he sees. He just sees and nothing more. The tears in his eyes have been sucked dry. His brain and heart have turned to stone. He sees an old man lying on the ground and he can't move. He is still alive. A tractor rumbles past, carrying a group of highly distressed and disoriented individuals. Some are seated while others stand, all in a state of frenzied turmoil, all screaming, crying and dying. A chain is dangling from under the vehicle and the old man takes hold of it. He is being dragged on the ground and is saturated in blood. A mother has lost her energy to run and throws her child away. An old woman finds the child, carries him on her shoulder running towards the border for almost twenty kilometres. A man with his sister in his arms is running and she is vomiting on her brother's shoulders. Vomiting blood and foam. A pink then red vomit. A man with his two daughters in his arms is running to the mountains. His two kids have already died red and black.

103

Omar reached his alleyway. There he saw a man falling on his two sons, and their mother two meters away from them, while stretching her hands toward them and screaming, her mouth has been frozen and her blood has slowed and turned to stone.

A few meters ahead, he saw an opened door of a house. He caught a fleeting glimpse, he saw a mother whose body was laid beside a furnace in the yard, and all his little children have already died of chemical gases. One of her daughters, out of panic, had gone inside the furnace.

On the stairs of the house he faced next, there has fallen a boy whose half body was inside, and the rest outside. He wanted to be sheltered indoors. His clothes were taken off, and his skin was blistered, his eyes swelled like two black balloons, and his hands dried as the branches of my tree. All Silent City was the platform of their theatre.

He went on. There was a little baby fallen on the ground. While crying, he walked four-leg to his mother. He lifted his mother's dress up and sucked his breasts. Instead of milk, a pink liquid was squirting. It sucked his life dry, and he died in his mother's bosom.

Out of breath and coughing intensely, he arrived home. He entered and saw all his seven daughters and his wife, who had risen from the dead, had passed away next to each other. He took his last breaths with his eyes closed. There came a faint cry of a child. Omar Kawar opened his eyes with a great effort. The child reached himself up the stairs. He was vomiting. Omar Kawar watched him. He couldn't believe his son was alive. Mohammad Shwan fell on the stairs and rolled down inside the alley.

He seems to be two years old. Kawar looks around. He finds himself at the middle of the theatre. Notices the photographers. Click . . . Click . . . Click . . . He feels two hands under his armpit then they drag him on the ground. They drop him down the stairs. They bring Mohammad Shwan and put him in his dead father's arms. Click . . . Click . . . Click . . . And it seems they died that way . . . Time and place is still frozen since that moments and everyone in the world and in Kurdewari believes in the poetic way they died.

There are no bombers now. The sky is thick with white smoke. It doesn't move. The prayers are gone. The photographers captured their photos and petrified their own countrymen. Dust, dust, dust . . . The city is grey. Five thousand people or five thousand one or so are now sleeping. Calm, quiet, and the city is silent now and its citizens are sleeping in a way that no one can wake them up. Some people are coming down the mountains towards the city. They have masks. Gunnies in their hands, they search every house. Full of gold and money and jewelries, clothes, furniture, and even spoons. They're leaving the city. No one is here now. It is just me and I just see. My feeling is dried up to dregs. I feel cold as razorblade. Cold like a stone on a mountain under the cold raindrops. I can't cry. I can't smile. I can't utter a single word. I am a dumb, silent, languageless song. I am deaf and dumb. The only place that can hold me now is my one and only oak tree. Taus, oh the god of the dead? Could you do something? Can you resurrect them now?

I walk into every alley and all I see is dead and burnt and lifeless bodies. The bowl of my eyes is creaking, like the creaking of an old wooden window which is opening.

22

The girl experiences an unusual sensation, recognizing that all these events have occurred for a purpose, perhaps a serendipitous one. She feels light-hearted and contemplates surrendering herself to the wind, akin to a small sparrow. Such a feeling is entirely new to her. The melodic singing of the Brothers of Time, accompanied by the resonating sounds of their Tembûrs, amplifies her unfamiliar emotions. As her gaze falls upon Resho's tomb, she envisions his paintings materializing upon it, transforming her into the final attendee of his exhibition.

Within this scene, a previously unseen painting emerges. Depicting a room surrounded by doorways leading to other chambers, it pulls the observer within, ensnaring them in its labyrinthine layers. Each of these confined spaces triggers memories of the girl's experiences with Resho: the exhibition, the Centre of Universe, the ardor of Tamura, the candle of his room, Tawuse Melek the god of Resho, their lovemaking, Resho's oak Tree, his repetitive dreams, and his unceasing writing.

In the painting, there are no figures or signs of life. The rooms, uniform in size yet distinct in color, beckon towards enigmatically shadowy realms. A grave occupies the foreground, a deep and ominous pit from which escape seems impossible, as if death itself resides there. The atmosphere imposes a profoundly perplexing sense of inevitability upon the viewer's gaze.

This is the realm of death—a manifestation of Resho's own mind, a haven that welcomed countless wandering souls stranded in the dark chasm of history. A history that confounded the people of Kurdewari, manipulated into rendering everyone a stranger in their own homeland. A history resembling a vortex, its purpose remaining unclear, draining the people's inner selves. This history blurred the lines between good and evil, patriot and traitor, slave and master for everyone.

Resho's mind was the sole sanctuary in which the dead could find solace, a haven within which they could peacefully rest. This painting could very well encapsulate the visual narrative of his entire life.

She craves for revealing the secret of her eyes; the secret of her life. She wants to remove the cover of her isolation and get to know where these inspirations are originated from. In this way, she can get relieved and nearer to Resho. After reading parts of his writings, she feels light like a feather, like a buoyant dandelion roaming inside the maze of Resho's mind. A feeling of curiosity drags her toward the Room of Inspiration. She would become Resho, feels that, if she reached the Cat in the window, if she saw, through the window, the high mountains, the oak jungle, and the girl under the oak tree.

The image of the window opening to the high mountains and the Cat which had mesmerized Resho has rooted in her mind. These not-in-this-world inspirations took Resho to the dark and pleasurable depths of death. The girl has admitted it, and she knows the path unto which these things culminate in, however, she still craves for realizing Resho's secret, a secret made of immortality. She decides to read the rest of his notebook in the Room of Inspiration.

She did not know that she would never be able to read Resho's second and third novel (or mine) if she ever happened to step inside the Room of Inspiration.

A black cloud has covered the sky, and so heavily does it rain that one could go up by grabbing the drops. Her long hair becomes broom of the cemetery. A pair of white and glittering eyes can be conspicuously seen. Her clothes mix with the darkness of the night, and only two bright spots are seen in the entirety of her body. Bit by bit, she approaches his house while her psyche is haunted by fear and anxiety. Resho's key is in her pocket, and she keeps fidgeting with it by her right hand, cannot take it out. The idea of taking the key out is overwhelming her mind. The door lock is put on a spell by a two-headed snake.

Today, she is agitated, so agitated.

All these scenes seem to her like being prepared and pre-planned for a day like today. The heavens and earth have been in complicity to bring her here, she thinks. Eventually, she takes the key out, closes her eyes, and opens the door.

She enters the yard. Through the mosaics, the roots of the oak tree have emerged. The pond is empty, and dried fish are stuck to the pond floor. The house has transformed into a graveyard, mirroring Resho's state of mind. In a secluded corner of the yard, ashes are piled. The wind and ashes dance hand in hand, soaring over the city's sky and settling on houses, yards, and balconies. Everywhere feels dream-like.

As she approaches the ashes, a feeling of assurance washes over her — Resho must have burned all his paintings. The remnants of wood and tar make it evident. She closes her eyes and screams from within and without. Her thumb beneath her other delicate fingers, she presses down so forcefully that it snaps. Surprisingly, the pain is muted. She stands senseless, resembling a stone on a mountain

She enters the house and ascends the stairs, a spiral pathway through time. She arrives in front of his room on the second floor, pausing for a moment before opening the door. Stepping inside, she avoids looking to her right, where the window is situated. She surveys the room, entirely crafted from wood. Half of the wall, reaching from floor to roof, is painted blue; its counterpart is adorned in red. The brown floor hosts three chairs and a blue desk. On the desk rests a green wine bottle, a packet of cigarettes, an upturned glass, and another filled with wine. Against the wall, a wedding dress hangs.

The room captivates the girl. She dares to gaze at the right side, where a white curtain conceals a portion of the room. With closed eyes, she moves the curtain aside and approaches the wall. Irresistibly, she

109

yearns to witness the window's view and the enigmatic black Cat. She opens her eyes with trepidation.

She sees nothing but a bare wall; a wall with its plasters removed by Resho so that he could smell the bricks. He used to dampen them.

He loved the smell of wet bricks.

The girl remains fixated on the wall, her gaze unwavering for a time. A procession of her sufferings parades before her eyes. Gradually, her illusions dissipate, and her eyes revert to their usual state. A sensation of weightlessness envelops her, akin to a feather carried by a gentle breeze. Returning to the room's center, she takes a seat on a chair, positioning her right hand beneath her chin. Her gaze intensifies as she fixates on the corner of the room before her. Her dark hair cascades, embracing the floor. With her left hand, she cradles her right wrist, determined to remain undistracted as she delves into contemplation and deep gazing.

23

I done poured my heart into finishin' this tale.

I scribbled 'bout that night me and Resho had over and over again. That quick but mighty black light, it's like a long and achin' dream. I saw all them departed from my homeland. They was like the cold, lifeless words of a tale no one's flippin' the pages of. Plus, I delved deep into them Omar Kawar stories, the ones Resho called that unfinished mission. I never mustered the nerve to edit 'em though. Still, somethin' feels missin', and I can't put my finger on it. I gotta keep startin' over from square one, again and again. I worked like a dog to wrap it up, even if I ain't seen that girl no more. I sure wish she could talk to me. I'd plead with her to share her words, but I wasn't keen on forcin' this tale into existence. When Resho passed on, I lost my ability to dream. He was right there in my dreams, part of me, stitched into my very existence. He was my whole dream. But I've penned so much 'bout Resho that, right now, even Tawuse Melek couldn't separate Resho from me.

An invisible hand was slippin' lines into my words every night, infusin' this tale with spirit, like that Sar Tarz Maqam liftin' up a soul.

I can't pinpoint when it's gonna go down, but I know it's a sure thing—Resho's words gonna mingle with the currents of the 'Sirwan' river. They'll drift back through the ages, ridin' the flow. They'll venture from them high mountain valleys to the charred oak jungles, and them oak trees, they'll be bloomin' once again. Crossin' borders, they'll dig deep into the earth, spreadin' through the land. Mountains, they'll stand even taller, and those oaks, they'll stretch further down in the dirt.

Maybe Resho's mission's 'bout remindin' all of us 'bout somethin'. Could be we gotta take a sec to recall, to see with new eyes, and to grasp what's happened to us.

24

Sirwan wanted to commit Resho's words to the water, but he gave it a second thought. He wanted to wait a bit longer. It was not yet the time for this story to be disseminated. He was utterly convinced that Resho's words would not reach the hearts of people because the doors of their hearts have been locked. He felt certain that they would suffocate the voice of this story. He knew well that it was not the right time, and I truly do admire him for that. He collected Resho's writings and added his own words, as well as those of the invisible hand (which is me, the mighty Taus), to the notebook. He wrapped it inside a green cloth and placed some oak leaves on it. Then, he went to Resho's grave and carefully looked at the white canvas covering it. With respect, he removed the canvas and dug the grave with his hands, as the girl had done with her petite hands and fingers. He reached Resho's body. The roots of his oak tree cradled Resho like a newborn baby. Sirwan caressed the roots, kissed Resho's hands, which were laid on his chest by the girl. He placed the story on Resho's body and looked at Resho's face for a while. Afterward, he went out and filled the grave with earth, leaves, and oaks.

Sirwan couldn't envision a life without Resho, yet he held the certainty that Resho would be reborn and his writing would resume. This understanding alleviated his concerns about Resho's writings and his own purpose, as he was confident they would blossom. It was not the right moment. Presently, no one can fully grasp the essence of my words.

25

Resho, why did not you understand? Why did you believe the story by which they have fooled people? Why did you write your dreams down without paying close attention to them? Why did not you think even for one moment that your dreams might be a part of their narrative? Why did not you dig more into your dreams? Why could not you unearth the truth? Why could not you, instead of opening their scars, breathe life into their shed blood and pains? You referred to them at some points but they were not enough Resho; I expected more of you Resho. I trusted you, Resho. I thought you might be a perfect choice, but . . . why did you turn the dead into numbers? Why did you make Omar Kawar the symbol of Silent City? Why did you overlook their pains? Why did not you mention the fact that each and every child could be a symbol? Why not old men? Why not old women? Why not those pregnant women whose infants died in their stomachs? Why not those who went blind due to the chemicals? Why did you reduce the Silent City to one person so that they could evade the whole truth and eliminate the reasons behind the bombardment? Why did not you mention the fact that the silent City paved the way for two countries to cease fire? Why did not you clearly write that the Silent City was made a sacrifice for the welfare and wellbeing of others? Why did not you say that that genocide was all a plan, a ridiculous but tragic theatre, an underhanded scenario written by the colonizers? Why did not you narrate the story of those malicious traitors who surrounded the city with guns, masks and vials? Why did you trust your dreams? Why did not you go to ask those who survived the bombardment and unearth the truth? To hear it from real witnesses? Oh Resho, you deserve a much more painful and burning death. You are going to be born again, to see, to, feel, and to suffer. Why did not you write that they bought the dead with filthy money? Why did not you write that those whose parents died by chemicals later received regular payments so they would forget about their own dead family? Why did they sell their dead sons, daughters . . . Why did they sell their dead mothers and fathers? Could money replace the warm hug of a mother? Could money replace the position of a father? No, no, no, never . . . So why did not you write about that? Why did not you talk about those who sought shelter in the neighbouring country, a country with a fake border which divided the Kurdish cities, lands, and villages? What happened to them? Why did not you say that they stole hundreds of kids? For what? To grow them up against their own people. To be trained as traitors. Why did not you write that hundreds of women were raped by soldiers and commanders of the country in which the victims took shelter? What about those children who died of hunger and thirst? What about those men who had to steal for bread? What about those soldiers who would eat before the eyes of starving refugees? Why did not you write that after the chemical bombardment the usurpers entered the city and stole people's money and jewelries? Why did not you mention those girls who asked for help from those who claimed to have freed the Silent City but, in return, they raped the frightened girls? Why did not you mention that they cut the dead women's arms and hands to steal their golden jewelries? Why did not you refer to suffocation of the Silent City's voice and the fact that only one leader was accused of the crime then he was immediately hanged? Why? So that he could not reveal the scheme for the genocide. Why were you so naïve and only wrote about your naïve dreams? What about that man who became blind after seeing all his family killed? Why did they leave him alone in that wild desert full of mines? From whom did he seek help? Who refused to help him? Why did not you mention that every Kurd and everyone in the oblivious world are responsible for the silence of the Silent City? Everyone in the Kurdewari should be in grief for them. Each and every one. Why do you think that being sad for the sake of those victims seems unjust? Everyone on this damn earth should be eternally sad. Only through sadness can a person come to know who he or she is. It is a death and revival cycle. Only in and through darkness can a person find light. Why did you dedicate only six narratives to narrate that horrific bombardment while thousands of stories are still impotent to narrate that dark day? Not enough . . . Not enough. Why did not you mention who is really responsible for this huge crime? Why did not you write about those thousands villages which were ruined? How many people were forced to leave their lives, their ancestral lands? What for? To migrate to cities and add to the population? Then what? Then they would become slaves of two nasty governments. Oh Resho, you are so damn fool. I will never ever forgive you. You will be sentenced to the most painful penalty. Why Resho, why? Your dead body should answer these questions. You are going to have to be born 1001 times on this earth to write about the truths of Silent City. In every Doon and façade in which you will be born, you will have to suffer again, you will have to be in grief, you will have to write again. I will take your loved ones away from you. No one and nothing should distract you. You will have to write and suffer and cry for them. You became the graveyard for more than two hundred thousand wandering souls but you could not pay them enough respect. That was not at all a decent way of welcoming them. Resho, you actually disrespected them. Your endeavors were fruitless, oh you the wretched Resho . . . What have you done? You said you would not throw away your words each of which could revive a dead homeless souls . . . I will never ever forgive you, Resho. You are the greatest unforgiven person on the face of this earth. But now you are dead? What can I do to you? You could have implemented your mission to the full extent . . . Why did not you give it more thoughts? Why did not you ask me? Why did you trust your dreams which had been formed and determined by their fake pictures and stories? Why did you trust yourself only? Why were you unaware of their manipulating power? Why did not you know that your conscious and unconscious mind is abundant with their pictures? With their stories? Why did not you understand that they even determined your and everybody's dream to make you all believe that it was only one leader and one country that martyred the Silent City? Why have you been so naïve? Why did you believe those who easily cheated you by their language and clothes? You never thought they could be the more insidious traitors, right? Why could not you differentiate between good and bad? So, everybody who speaks in a standard way is a good person, huh? So you thought that the chemical bombardment was the result of war, right? Huh? Why did not think that could be just a theatre? Some people came inside the city right after the bombardment and then cheated and manipulated the minds of the world. Just by some photos. Why did not you tear down your writings? Why did not you think they could be all lies? Again, from the heart of death, you will be born again. This time, at another corner of Kurdewari, you will die and come back to life many times during a fortnight, until you lose your senses and feelings. Then, you will be as cold as a stone upon a mountain, enduring rain, snow, and the blazing of fire. You will have to observe only.

26

A whirlwind opens the window ...